The Bard of Tilbury

The Talisman - Book IV

The Bard
of
Tilbury

Michael Harling

iv

Lindenwald Press

To Mitch and Charlie
Without whom there would be no story.

Also by Michael Harling

The Postcards Trilogy
Postcards From Across the Pond
More Postcards From Across the Pond
Postcards From Ireland

The Talisman Series
The Magic Cloak
The Roman Villa
The Sacred Tor

Finding Rachel Davenport

OPENING

Stratford-Upon-Avon
21 June 2016

To Franklin Wyman,

You do not know me, but I was a friend of your late cousin (once removed), Annie. As executor of her will, it was I who transferred her estate to you. I was instructed, however, to keep the enclosed items until this date. They include: one manuscript, two quill pens and three groat coins, each worth four pence in Tudor times.

They were discovered on the 15th of October 1630 among the papers of John Heminges, a close associate of Mr. William Shakespeare. They were carefully preserved, stored away and, eventually, forgotten.

They were rediscovered in 1851 by workmen renovating a manor house, and then

passed down through the family of that
house until they were bought in an estate
auction by Miss Annie McAllister in 1955.

It was Miss McAllister's wish that
they be delivered to you on this date.

You may do as you like with the
manuscript and the coins. She indicated to
me that you would know what to do with the
quills.

Yours Sincerely,

Colonel Merrick, RAF (retired)
Executor for the estate of Miss McAllister

PREFACE

My name is Mitch, and I'm a scribe. That means I can write. This isn't unusual where I come from, but in England, at the time I am writing this, it's something special, so they call you something special, like 'Scribe.' At least that's what William Shakespeare told me.

Maybe I'd should explain.

Where I come from is four-hundred and twenty-eight years in the future, this being the year 1588. In my time, I live in Wynantskill, New York, with my brother Charlie, where—a few years ago—our grandfather sent us a magic cloak. Naturally, we didn't believe it was magic (that's not something we're familiar with in our time), but then we found ourselves in the year 517. And it was the cloak that took us there.

Fortunately, it took us back too.

Now, every year, our grandfather sends us another gift, and the cloak takes us—and the gift—back in time, to the town where Granddad lives. Or, to where he will live one day. I'm not really sure how it works, or why we always go there, it's just the way it is. It's all a little strange, and I'm still not sure if these are just dreams, or if we are really and truly there. I guess that depends on whether you believe in magic cloaks or not. And I'm not saying I definitely do, but sometimes I think that makes more sense than any alternative theory.

This gift, like all the others, came in the summer, during those awkward weeks when Charlie and I are both the same age. It's a ritual that has been going on for four years, so we were kind of expecting it, but to be honest, we weren't looking forward to it. Both Charlie and I were hoping the gifts would stop because, last year, we got shields and that seemed like fun, but then we ended up fighting in the battle of Hastings and that wasn't fun at all. In fact, it scared us so much we decided we wouldn't use the cloak again.

But then the gifts came, and they were just feathers, and Charlie pointed out that we wouldn't be in much danger if we went to a place where they used feathers, so we decided to try the cloak again. The only problem was, our mother had taken the cloak from us as punishment for us taking the cloak back from her after she had taken it from us the year before. It's complicated, and has to do with our grandfather "abandoning" us, which is what she calls his moving to England.

Although that's sort of fair, taking our cloak isn't, but when we appealed to our father, she told him (quite rightly) that we were fifteen years old and too old to be playing with a cloak. But this year, our father finally grew a pair, and told her (quite rightly) that we were fifteen years old and could jolly well decide for ourselves what we wanted to play with. Only he didn't say "jolly," and that shocked Mom into giving up the cloak, but only because we'd gotten feathers. If we ever got anything more dangerous, she told us, she'd take it back, as if it would be our fault if we did.

So, that night, after our mother and father went to sleep, we got up, dressed by the light of the full moon, and laid down on my bed, side by side, holding the feathers. Then we covered ourselves with the cloak and went to sleep. I know that sounds dumb but that's how it works.

And it worked again this year, and this is what happened.

ACT I

SCENE I
Near the village of Horsham, Sussex, England

CHARLIE

We woke up in a field of wheat.

I'm going to tell this part of the story because it was down to me that we had any sort of adventure at all. If it had been left up to Mitch, we'd have simply had a look around and gone back home. Although, if we had done that, we wouldn't have ended up in the army and almost killed in a rebellion, so I guess it depends on your point of view.

It was nice in the field. The sky was grey, but the air was warm, and a soft breeze ruffled the tops of the wheat. The wheat wasn't very tall or very brown, so I figured it was sometime during the summer, though what year it was remained a mystery. The only thing I did know was that we needed to get out of the field as soon as possible, before a farmer saw us crushing his crops. So, while Mitch had a cautious look to make sure the coast was clear, I used a rock to cut an X deep into the soil. Then we folded the cloak so we could carry it and ran, as straight as we could, to the edge of the field, where we made an arrow out of rocks pointing toward the X I had made. This was our trail of breadcrumbs, so we could find our way back home.

We were pretty sure we'd appeared in the same spot as usual, and that was confirmed when we found a rutted dirt track at the edge of the field and a farmhouse nearby. The house and surrounding yard didn't look much different from the last time we'd seen it. There was more junk in the yard and different outbuildings, but nothing that provided any more clues as to what year it was than the wheat did. I didn't see anyone, though there were signs of activity—the sound of chopping wood, a door slamming, a voice calling, and smoke rising from a chimney sticking out of the thatched roof.

"There," I said, pointing.

Mitch looked. "What?"

"The chimney. There was no chimney in that house—or anywhere—last time we were here."

Mitch nodded. "So, it's later than last time. I hope that means they're more advanced."

"Well, they have chimneys, but it doesn't look like they've got indoor plumbing."

We hurried on before someone saw us. Strangers drew people's curiosity, and strangers dressed as strangely as we were drew a lot of curiosity, and if we had learned anything from our previous adventures, it was that being taken notice of generally ended badly.

As expected, the lane we were on soon led to a wider road. Unexpectedly, however, we saw houses there—about a dozen stone and wood structures, some with smoke seeping through thatched roofs and a few with crude chimneys. There were people, as well. A woman, wearing the usual burlap-bag-style clothing, hauled a bucket of water across a cluttered yard while two children—with bare feet and dressed in what looked like rags—followed, each carrying a load of firewood. Outside a different house, a man wearing a wide-brimmed, floppy hat looked our way. He was dressed in a loose shirt, baggy pants, and knee-length leather boots, which contrasted sharply with our jeans, sneakers, tee shirts and light, denim jackets. And that's before you take into account the cloak we were carrying.

He looked our way and shouted something, which made the woman look up and cry out in surprise. Pretending we hadn't heard, we turned away and hurried down the road that led to the village of Horsham. By now it was a familiar trip. We recognized the stone bridge and the area where the Roman villa had been, but the land had changed from forests and overgrown meadows to fields bordered by low stone walls and an occasional house. Fortunately, there were few people about, and we kept our heads down as we walked, adhering to the "if we can't see them, they can't see us" theory. Incredibly, that seemed to work, because no one challenged us along the road (which was in a shocking state), and soon we caught sight of a large dwelling that we took to be Steric's public house. It had been there since our first visit, but now the building had a second story, a slate roof, timber and brick walls, and a new sign nailed to a post out front that read "The Green Dragon." We were glad to see it because it marks the edge of the village and tells us where we have to turn.

There are many reasons for not going into Horsham (or any medieval village, for that matter): the muck on the road is ankle-deep, it smells like an open sewer, and people tend to stare at us. But that's not why we turned away. We turned because we were going somewhere else.

Pendragon's house (or the house Pendragon used to live in) was the only place we knew of, so that's where we always went, even though it was also where the trouble always started.

"This time, we're just going to have a look," Mitch told me. "We'll see what's there, then we'll go back to the wheat field and return home. Deal?"

I don't like when he tries to tell me what to do, but I wasn't in a hurry to repeat last year's adventure, so I shook his hand and said, "Deal."

As it turned out, by the time we got to where the house was supposed to be—having had to bull our way through thickets of brambles and walls of weeds—I started to think there had been no need for our agreement because there was nothing there.

This was a surprise. Even though it had been built by the Romans (and who knew how long ago that had been), when we last saw it, in 1066, Pendragon's great-great to the Nth degree grandson, Aelric, had been living there, and it had been in fairly good shape. He'd even built an extension and fixed the door. So, to find it in ruins was disappointing.

You could still—just barely—tell that a house had been there. Remnants of the stone walls surrounding the yard, nearly invisible beneath a mass of moss and weeds, were still in place, and glimpses of grey flint peeked through the greenery. We pushed the weeds aside, located the gap where the front gate had been, and headed toward the house.

It was a short distance, but completely overgrown, and by the time we got to the front door, our hands were covered in scratches and a fog of insects was swarming around our heads. The house walls had long ago collapsed and were only shoulder high in some places, and the interior was a jumble of beams, rotting thatch and damp vegetation. We picked our way

12

through the ruin—often having to squirm under or climb over beams, with Mitch still clutching the cloak—until we found the back wall. There, a section of the roof was almost intact, making a small area of shade where the weeds thinned out. This had been the dining area, and even though neither of us said anything, we both knew what we were looking for, and it was Mitch who found it.

He scraped away layers of dirt and rotted leaves, kicked aside some fallen stones and uncovered the corner of a wooden plank. Together we dug a bit more, revealing a portion of the big oak slab, still remarkably solid, that Pendragon and Aerlic had used for a table. Wiping the mud away, we located the carving, its grooves, packed with damp earth, clearly showing the outline of an airplane (though it looked more like a fancy cross) that Mitch had carved into it the first time we had been there.

We stared at it for a few minutes. Mitch ran a finger around it, tracing the cuts he had made, then we silently buried it again.

"That's proof," Mitch said. "This is definitely the place, and there definitely isn't anything here."

"Do you supposed this is to tell us the adventures are over?"

Mitch looked around at the desolation. "It could be. But right now, I think we ought to head back."

"Home?"

Mitch nodded.

"Okay," I said, feeling more relief than I let on.

We began retracing our steps, and when we got to the middle of the room, where the fire pit used to be, we heard a voice.

"Is anyone home?"

We froze.

The voice came again. "Hello?"

Mitch leaned close. "What should we do?"

I shrugged. The voice wasn't gruff or threatening. In fact, it sounded lilting, like a child's.

"Let's go see," I said, stepping forward before Mitch could stop me.

I went to the doorway. Standing in the path we had made through the weeds was a young boy. He was small and slim, wearing a short jacket and long pants—both worn and dusty—and carrying a bundle made from a tattered blanket. A red felt cap, with red hair poking out from beneath it, was pulled low over the brow of his slender face. When he saw me, his face, which was already pale, turned paler still.

"Who—," he began. Then Mitch came up beside me, carrying the cloak. When the boy saw him, his eyes widened, his jaw dropped, and he went so white I thought he might faint. "It's you," he said, taking a shambling step backward.

I held my hands in front of me to show we meant him no harm.

"It's all right," I said. "We're—"

"The knights," he said, pointing a shaking finger at us. "The wanderers, the Guardians." He looked closer at Mitch. "The cloak!" He dropped his bundle and slumped into a sitting position, still staring at us, gasping as he tried to speak. "The legends … passed from mother to daughter … and son. I thought them fairy tales … but it is you … the brothers who appeared to my kinsman, Aelric … and Pendragon before him."

I stepped forward, still holding my hands up, feeling almost as dizzy as the boy looked. After Pendragon, I could understand meeting Aelric—he lived in the same

14

house, after all—and I didn't doubt they'd pass stories down about us, and stories tended to grow grander over time, so I could sorta understand why they kept calling us knights, but if this kid really was a relation of Aelric, where did he come from?

"Who are you?" I asked, trying to sound friendly.

"Nicholas," the boy said, "Nicolas Fen. I live many days north of here."

Mitch stepped up beside me. "Then what are you doing here?"

"Traveling" Nicholas said. Slowly, and still shaking, he rose to his feet. "I was on the road to London but was overcome by a strong urge to see where my forefathers came from. And now I understand why."

"Your forefathers," I said. "You mean Pendragon?"

Nicholas nodded. "And Aelric, the Wanderer. This was his home until he was forced out. He settled in the north, on the eaves of Fishwick. Our family prospered, but many generations have spread our fortune thin. My father is a farmer outside the village of Preston."

"And you," Mitch said, "a boy so young, traveling on your own?"

Nicholas puffed out his chest and took a step toward us. "I am fourteen summers," he said, "nearly a man."

"Well, we're fifteen," I said, "and that doesn't count as an adult where we come from."

Nicholas looked puzzled. "You seem as men: tall and sound as father's horse. From where to you hail?"

I glanced at Mitch and shrugged. "Wynantskill," I said.

Nicolas shook his head. "I have heard of no such place."

I sighed. "I don't doubt it."

15

"But you are here," Nicolas continued, "for a reason, and I am here for a reason. We must have been meant to meet."

"I don't know about that," Mitch said. "We're not even sure why we're here."

"You are the Guardians, the knights of old, you have come to save——"

"We're just boys," I said, "like you. Nothing special, except we keep being brought here. But we never know why."

"So, I must be your reason," Nicolas said, his face beaming. "Come with me to London. We will find adventure there, and riches."

"I think we'd rather go back home," Mitch said, giving me a hard stare. "That's what we've agreed to."

"You can't, you mustn't," Nicholas said, his voice rising even higher. "You've just appeared. I saw you, coming from the house of Aelric, like angels from heaven."

"We didn't actually appear in——," I began, but Nicolas cut me off.

"You have a purpose here, you do, and I …" He shook his head and covered his face with his hands. "Coming here was a risk, a huge risk. I have no paper, I might have been arrested, or fallen victim to scoundrels of the highway. I used the last of my food and coin because I knew in my heart I had to be here. Then you appeared, the answer to my prayers, and now you want to turn away …"

"Listen," Mitch said, "we don't know you, we don't know why we're here or what we're doing. I think it will be safer for all of us if we just go back home."

Nicolas balled his hands into fists and dropped them to his side, revealing a face contorted with rage.

"You'd leave me to starve, or be picked off by scalawags? You'd see me in jail? You can't be knights, you have no honour."

I saw now that he wasn't as enraged as he was frightened. He seemed to be struggling to keep himself from crying. I stepped forward, embarrassed for him, and placed a hand on his shoulder.

"Take it easy, buddy, everything will be all right."

He knocked my hand off and wiped fiercely at his eyes. "No, it won't! You'd see me jailed, or … or …"

"Why are you so afraid of jail? You haven't done anything wrong, have you?"

"I have no paper," he said, his voice rising again.

"Paper?"

"Permission to travel. If I am found out—"

"You need permission to travel?"

This caught him off guard, and he began to calm down.

"Of course. Don't you?"

"Not where we come from. But if we need papers to travel here, I think it best we leave, don't you?"

"But in a group, we will be more secure, and anonymous. I travelled with a group of merchants to London but left them to come here. We could find other people on our way back. We would blend in."

I stepped back and ran a hand down my jacket and jeans. "Not in these clothes. We'd only draw attention to you, and us."

"But I could vouch for you. I could say we were performers, and that they are your costumes."

"Performers? Of what?"

For the first time, he smiled. "I will show you." He looked at the brambles surrounding us. "But not here. Near the river, where the land is open."

17

"Charlie," Mitch said. "That's not a good idea."

"There's one of him and two of us," I said. "If he tries anything, we can take him."

Nicolas picked up his bundle and turned away. I followed him out to the river where the ground was more open, hoping Mitch would come too. Nicolas put his bundle down, stepped to a flat area and waited until Mitch grudgingly arrived.

Without any fanfare, or preparation, Nicolas jumped up and did a back flip and then a forward flip, spinning through the air and landing on his feet, making it look effortless.

"That's all well and good," Mitch said, "but we can't do that, and although I'm not sure why we're here, I'm sure it's not to do that."

Nicolas looked crestfallen again, and I was afraid he might have another melt down.

"Look," I said, "we'll make a deal with you."

"Charlie …," Mitch said.

I ignored him and pulled the feather out of my pocket.

"This is what we came here with. Does this look like anything useful to you? Will this protect us on the road? Will this keep us out of trouble?"

"This isn't what we agreed," Mitch said.

"What's the harm? It's just a feather." I held it out to Nicolas. "Tell us how this could possibly help us, and we'll come with you."

Nicolas took the feather, staring at it with open awe. "This is a writing quill." He looked at me, then at Mitch. "Do you know your letters?"

"You mean, can we read and write?" I asked.

Nicolas nodded.

"Of course we can," I said.

"Then we are rich."

"What are you talking about?" Mitch asked.

"We can find other travellers," Nicolas said, stroking the feather, "and I will perform for them. When a crowd gathers, you can offer your services. People will want letters read. And written."

"And they'll pay for that?" I asked.

"Handsomely," Nicolas said.

Mitch stepped forward. "Charlie, we agreed."

I drew a breath. My mouth was dry, and my stomach felt like ice. "Yes, we did," I said. Then I looked at Nicolas and saw his eyes, a dusty green, shining with excitement and hope, and felt a warmth begin to glow in my chest. "But I made a promise."

SCENE II

On the London Road

MITCH

I was plenty mad at Charlie for a while, but then I realized that running back home almost as soon as we arrived would have been a stupid thing to do. And Nicolas—even though he was a strange little guy— proved to be as good as his word. He helped us fit in better (though not much) by giving Charlie his hat, and me another one he pulled from his bundle. And he showed me a new way to fold and carry the cloak, turning it inside-out and tying it in a way that made it resemble the bundle he was carrying, which helped us become even less conspicuous than the floppy hats he gave us.

We left Horsham the way Nicolas had arrived, along a path that led through empty fields and dense woodland, meaning we saw no one until we reached the road. It was the same one we had marched to London on the last time we'd been there, but it was in worse shape. There were also more people—groups of four to a dozen or more, walking or pushing carts— though all of them were heading south.

What we needed, Nicolas told us, was a group going north, so we started walking, hoping to catch up with one. After a while, when we didn't find anyone going our way, we decided to sit by the side of the road and wait.

It was then that Nicolas put his plan into action.

"A group comes," he said, pointing. "Large. Ten or more. And wealthy."

"How do you know?" Charlie asked.

"They have a horse pulling their cart," Nicolas said, rising and stepping onto the road.

When they got close, he did a back flip, then a cartwheel and a round-off that he used to spring into a forward flip. He landed in the middle of the road in front of the startled horse.

"Would you care to tarry and enjoy some entertainment?"

"Away," the lead man—wearing a cloak, a wide brimmed hat, and an impatient expression—said. "We are in haste and have no time for tricks." He waved Nicolas out of the way, but Nicolas stayed where he was.

"Then do you have letters to write, or documents to read?" He bowed and swept a hand toward us. "My friends are scribes. They are at your service."

"I am a lawyer's clerk," the man said. "I know my letters well enough. Away with you."

This time, Nicolas did step aside, still smiling, and inclining his head at each of the travellers as they passed. The last one, a man wearing a long, leather coat, which looked out of place on such a warm day, put a hand in his pocket drew it out and flicked it toward Nicolas.

"Beggars," he said, as a few coins clinked onto the stones.

Nicholas bowed low, then picked them up as the man passed.

"I told you we could make a fortune," Nicholas said, holding the coins out to us, his face beaming.

"But he called us beggars," I said. "That's insulting."

Nicholas looked at me through narrowed eyes. He was no longer beaming. "If beggars we be, then we cannot afford to feel slighted." He closed his fist over the coins. "Would you rather we buy bread, and live another day, or shall I throw these away for the sake of your pride?"

I looked around. There was not a sole—much less a convenience store—in sight, but I didn't think Nicholas would thank me for pointing this out, so I just shook my head and folded my arms. "Sorry," I said. Nicholas nodded, accepting my apology, but when he came to sit with us, he sat next to Charlie, as far from me as he could.

A few other groups passed by, all heading south. Although Nicolas did his best to entice them, they mostly ignored us, not even bothering to throw coins our way. Only one traveller took up our offer to read— a young man, dusty and bedraggled from the road, with a letter of introduction, as well as a document allowing him permission to travel. He was anxious to know, before he arrived at his new place of employment, what it actually said. He didn't seem embarrassed that he couldn't read, and happy to pay me to do it for him.

Although I could read, it was still hard going, at least at first. The pages were creased and dirty, and the ink smeared in places. Also, the language may have been English, but they spelled the words funny, and they didn't always spell them the same way. "Bridle" could be spelled "brydeal" or "brydell" or "byrdyl" even in the same paragraph. But once I figured out the words were spelled phonetically, it got easier. The man offered money once I finished. I didn't want to take it, but Nicolas insisted.

After that, the sun sank low, the traffic stopped, and I began to realize that Nicolas intended to stay there all night. As darkness approached, we sheltered under some shrubs, made a bed out of grass and leaves, and covered ourselves with the cloak and a tattered blanket from Nicolas's bundle. We had no fire, or food, and had to huddle together for warmth, but Nicolas, who bedded down next to Charlie, remained maddeningly optimistic.

In the morning, we drank from a nearby stream, washed in the stunningly cold water, then returned to the roadside to wait.

It didn't take long. The sun had barely risen when a group approached, heading north, and Nicolas hailed them. This time, he didn't do any acrobatics, or offer our services, he just asked if we might travel with them. And they agreed. So, we walked with them, carrying our bundles, and soon met other travellers who also joined us, until we numbered about thirty people, spread along the highway in a loose group. Nicolas did a few of his acrobatic tricks, but not for money. He was just showing off and using it as an excuse to explain our strange appearance, claiming we were a group of performers in costume. After a while, no one seemed to mind how we were dressed, and once they found out we could read and write, they started asking for our services.

I read a few documents as we walked, and when we stopped for lunch, Nicolas bought some ink from one of the merchants, and I began writing letters, as well. By then, we had enough money for food, which put me in a better mood, even though I seemed to be the only one who was working. During our down time, and when we finally stopped for the night, Charlie spent all his time with Nicolas, who was teaching him acrobatic moves, leaving me to do all the letter reading and writing.

At night, there were fires, and we were able to warm ourselves while Nicolas and, increasingly, Charlie, entertained the growing band of travellers. I had to admit, Nicolas had come through for us. As he had predicted, we were safer, and more anonymous, in the larger group. We earned money, we bought provisions, I got better at medieval reading and writing, Charlie got better at jumping around like an idiot and, four days after setting out, we made it to the outskirts of London.

SCENE III

A street in London

CHARLIE

We could smell London before we saw it. It wasn't like last time, when we were close enough to see the grey haze that clung to the horizon, and occasionally catch a whiff of smoke when the wind was right. This time, the stench of sewage, rotting meat and greasy smoke wafted our way well before we saw the haze.

When I pointed this out to Nicholas, the detail he keyed in on was that we had been to London before, not that it smelled like a septic tank. In fact, he didn't even seem to notice, and neither did anyone else we were travelling with.

"Really," he asked, his eyes alight. "You've been to London? And you never told me?"

"Well, no," I said. "We just saw it, like now. We went around it."

"You were this close to London and you didn't go?" He asked this as if we had been offered gold and refused to take it.

"We didn't have a choice."

Then I told him how me and Mitch, and his ancestor, Aelric, had marched to join Harold's army, and in just seven days, had made it to York, where we fought the Vikings. He was dead impressed, so I didn't tell him about how we had nearly died from exhaustion and only made it because an old Druid had taken us in his cart rather than leave us to die by the side of the road. And that made me wonder: would the old Druid—known as Malcolm the last time we had seen him—show up again to save us? If he did, he wouldn't be coming any time soon. We weren't in the most enviable position, but I knew from experience that things could (and probably would) get much worse before they were dire enough for the old Druid to come to our rescue. Just once I wished he would show up early and tell us what we were supposed to do. But there was no sense wishing for something I knew would never happen.

I didn't tell Nicolas any of this. The story of our march and the battle left him awe-struck, and I thought it best to keep it that way.

To enter London, we had to pass through a cluster of houses and farmland, and a densely populated area they called Suthuk, even though a signpost outside of the settlement read, "Southwark." One by one, our travel companions began to peel off, going to their respective destinations, leaving us exposed and in a hurry to enter the anonymity of the city. Although Southwark was small it was crowded, and soon people began to notice our clothes and call out to us, demanding to know who we were, where we were from and why we were dressed like that.

Nicholas told the story about us being performers, but all that did was focus their suspicions.

"Actors," one man said, managing to spit at the same time.

"Thieves," said another.

"Pay them no heed," Nicholas said quietly. "People

are wary of travellers, but we are safe enough."

That didn't ease my apprehension, and Nicholas stopping to pick up a stray piece of wood to use as a walking stick—or a weapon—only increased my unease. We put our heads down and walked a little faster. As we neared the river, the streets became narrow and cramped and the buildings more packed and ramshackle. It also began to smell worse, and I hoped getting to the river would ease the stench, but that seemed to be where most of it was coming from. It was brown and sludgy and packed with boats of all sizes. Men shouted, animals brayed and mooed and howled, and the confusion might have been annoying except it kept people from worrying about us.

The road led us to something that looked like a small castle at the head of a busy street stretching across the water. It was made of stone, with turrets at each corner and a huge archway in the middle that the road went through. It dwarfed the nearby houses, but was itself dwarfed by some of the structures on the bridge, which reached four or five stories into the smoky air.

At the top of the castle, poking up like porcupine quills, were tall spikes, each with a head stuck to its end. Some were so old they were practically skulls while others were fresh and still dripping blood. Mitch saw them first and pointed them out to Nicolas, who just shrugged.

"Thieves, traitors," Nicolas said. "That's what they do to their heads."

We didn't want to know what they did with the rest of them, so we just walked fast until we passed through the archway and got onto the bridge. If I hadn't been aware of the river rushing below us, I wouldn't have thought we were anywhere other than a crowded, smelly street. It was lined with houses, many of which hung perilously over the edge, daring gravity to pull them into the water. And just like any other street, there were people pushing, shouting, carrying loads, riding horses, bargaining, calling out to passers-by about their wares, and, of course, street performers.

Naturally, Nicolas was most interested in the performers. Some walked on stilts, others played strange-looking guitars, juggled burning sticks, or recited poetry. For the most part, people ignored them, but every now and again someone would drop a coin in their outstretched caps. It gave us a hopeful feeling.

When we finally got into the city of London, we found it wasn't as bad as Southwark; it was worse. The lanes were cramped and crowded and lined with wooden buildings stacked haphazardly on top of one another, looking in danger of collapse. Despite it being a sunny day, and just past noon, hardly any light filtered down to street level—though much of the heat did—making it feel like we were walking through a dark, sweltering canyon. To keep from gagging, I had to breathe through my mouth, but it didn't seem to bother Nicolas. He gaped at the buildings, his mouth open, his eyes wide.

"It's wonderful," he said, "magnificent. Can you believe we are really here?"

I looked at the people in ragged clothes, pushing carts, carrying sacks, bent and straining, staring down at the muck-covered cobbles.

"No," I said. Mitch just shook his head, looking like he wanted to throw up.

Nicholas grabbed my arm. "This is where we will make our fortunes," he said, tugging me forward.

"Come. We'll begin now. We have only half a day to earn enough for food and lodging."

"I've got money," Mitch said.

"Not enough," Nicolas said leading us deeper into the labyrinth of lanes. "We must find a crowd where we can gain an audience. Be ready with your quill, Mitch."

For an agonizingly long time, I thought we would never find what Nicholas was looking for. We went down lanes, squeezed through alleyways—Nicholas called them ginnels—and even through the back passages of the hovels lining the streets. At every turn, we saw nothing but walls and slivers of grey sky. Then suddenly we came to an open area surrounding the biggest church I have ever seen.

It was longer than a football field and about four times as tall as the nearby buildings. And that was just the main part. From the centre rose a tower, easily doubling its height, with a strangely unimpressive spire sprouting from its square top. We later learned that the original, much more impressive, spire had been struck by lightning and burned down years before, and there hadn't been enough money to fix it, but at that time all our attention was focused on the crowd.

The churchyard—for that was what it was—teemed with people, walking to and fro, standing and chatting, bargaining, buying, selling. I didn't need Nicholas to tell me that this was what he had been searching for, because among the waves of humanity were street performers. We waded into the crowd and located an empty spot well away from any competition. Nicholas put down his bundle and his walking stick and went into his act. At his insistence, I joined in, doing some back flips and somersaults. No one was impressed, but they were impressed with Nicolas. He had some stunningly good moves and soon we had a little money, but Nicolas told us it wasn't enough for a decent dinner and a place to stay, so we kept at it.

Mitch offered his services to the crowd, but there didn't seem to be as much need for someone to read and write as there had been when we were on the road.

Then a trio of boys who were juggling wooden clubs spotted us and one of them began walking our way.

"This could be trouble," Nicolas said. "They might not like us taking customers away from them."

But the boy, who was tall and lanky, didn't seem angry. His clothes, which looked about three sizes too small for him, strained at the elbows as he placed his hands on his hips, studying each of us with a sly smile.

"You're not bad," the boy said to Nicolas. "I'm Arthur, and they are my partners, Robert and Alfred." He pointed to his companions, still juggling for the amusement of the crowd.

Nicolas eyed him warily. "I'm Nicolas, and these are my friends, Charlie and Mitch."

Arthur looked me up and down. "What were you playing at?" I assumed he meant my acrobatics.

"I'm just learning," I said. "I'll get better."

Arthur laughed. "You'd better, if you like to eat." Then he turned to Mitch. "And what do you do?"

"He can read and write," Nicolas said.

"Hey," I cut in. "So can I."

Nicolas and Arthur ignored me.

"He can read documents for people, or write letters for them," Nicolas said. "For a fee."

Arthur rubbed his chin. "Hmm, how much have you made today."

"Enough," Nicolas said. "We are able to take care of ourselves."

Arthur nodded to his friends. "We belong to a guild," he said. "There are many of us all over the city. We live together and pool our money, and if you join us, you'll be guaranteed food and a place to sleep, in exchange for your earnings."

That idea sounded good, too good. On the other hand, food and shelter might not be a bad thing. Arthur continued to smile, but Nicholas shook his head. "We prefer to work alone. Thank you for your kind offer, but we have no interest in joining you."

Arthur stepped close to Nicolas and looked down at him. "I think it would be better if you did."

Alfred and Robert now joined us, carrying their juggling clubs under their arms. They stood on either side of us. The one called Alfred was short and stocky, with unruly black hair and a red scar across his cheek. Robert was lanky, and gazed at us with dark, penetrating eyes.

"Look," Arthur said, holding his hands up, palms out. "I'm not going to force you to join us. We'll come looking for you in a couple of days, though. After a few nights on the streets, you'll be begging us to take you in." He dropped his hands and gave us a humourless grin. "But by then we may not want you."

Nicolas took a step back. "We'll take that chance. We want to work on our own—"

Arthur grabbed Nicolas by the arm and dug a thumb into his bicep. Nicolas squeezed his eyes shut against the pain but didn't cry out. I took a step forward to help him but felt a strong hand on my shoulder. Two other boys came out of the crowd and stood behind us.

"You're wiry, but strong," Arthur said, releasing him and pushing him away. Nicolas massaged his arm but said nothing. "After a few days without food, though, you won't be jumping around so spritely." Arthur crossed his arms. "Don't be foolish. Come with us. We'll take care of you. You'll have a roof over your heads and food in your bellies. And we'll teach you. You'll earn a lot more money."

Still Nicolas shook his head. "I don't know …"

I shrugged the hand off my shoulder and stepped close to Nicholas. "What harm can it do?" I said, bending close to his ear. "And besides, I don't think we have a choice."

"Your friend speaks sense," Arthur said.

Several more boys came out of the crowd, forming a circle around us.

Nicolas sighed and leaned over to pick up his bag and walking stick. Arthur stepped on the stick. "You won't be needing that," he said. "It's not far, where we're going."

Mitch picked up the inside-out cloak, and the three of us stood side-by-side, with Nicholas in the middle. Arthur smiled and looked at the boys surrounding us. "Say hello to our new partners."

The boys nodded. Nicolas looked glum. We fell into line with Arthur leading and the rest of the boys following behind.

SCENE IV

A Lodging House in London

MITCH

They led us through the city to where the streets were even more narrow and crooked, and where the houses that rose from the muck had each floor sticking out a little further over the one below, leaving us in perpetual twilight. Here, people were lying in the streets along with the filth, and children in rags huddled next to the buildings, begging for food. This made me glad we would have a place to stay that evening, but like Nicolas, I was getting a bad feeling. The boys following us kept close, ready to catch us if we tried to run. That thought never entered my mind, however. Where would I run to?

After they'd marched us around for a while, we arrived at the edge of the city. At least I assumed it was the edge, because there was a wall in front of us. You could hardly see it, though, because it was almost completely covered by the ramshackle buildings stacked up against it. Arthur led us into one—a broad building made of warped boards and rough-hewn beams—and we followed him up a rickety staircase to a dim corridor. There, he stopped in front of a door and rapped out a series of knocks. A small window on the door flicked open and closed, then the door creaked, and a rasping voice came through the gap.

"Why are you back so soon?"

"We brought new recruits," Arthur said.

"Who told you to drag urchins in from the street? I will tell you—"

"They're fresh."

The voice faltered. "Are you certain?"

"Just in from the country today."

The door swung open and a fat man with a pudgy, unshaven face stepped into view. He was dressed in ragged clothes and had a round cap pulled low over his head, making his straggly grey hair stand out. He looked down at Nicholas, then up at me and Charlie.

"Recruits, eh?" he said, addressing Arthur though he kept his eyes on us. "What can they do?"

"They're acrobats," Arthur said, pointing at Nicolas. "This one is, anyway." Then he pointed at Charlie. "This one thinks he is, and this one." He pointed at me. "Says he can read and write."

"A scholar, eh?" the man said. "We have little use for that here."

"Perhaps he has other talents," Arthur said.

The man scowled at me. "Perhaps. But he doesn't look the type. And why are they dressed like that?"

"That's their costumes," Nicolas said.

"Eh. Well, we've no use for them, either." The man looked at Arthur. "What have they made."

Arthur nudged Nicolas, who held out a few coins. The man glared at him.

"We only came to town this afternoon," Nicolas said.

"Well, you'd better come back with more than this in the future," the man said. "I don't run a charity here." He snatched the coins from Nicolas. "Come inside then. Arthur will get you settled."

The man retreated into the room, and we followed. The room was large, cluttered and lit by a single candle on a table in the corner. Heaps of clothing and blankets were piled against one wall. Stacked near another were plates and cups and candle sticks and picture frames and buckets and bottles and more. Many of the items reflected the glow of the candle, making the pile sparkle.

"I'm Lovell," the man said, as he waddled to the table. "I will be your mother, your father, your master, and God almighty as long as you are here. Is that understood?"

"Yes," Nicolas said without enthusiasm. Charlie and I chimed in, as well.

"Good," Lovell said. "I will provide you with a roof over your head and see that you have food in your bellies, as long as you stay profitable."

He didn't say what would happen if we didn't, but the image of the children in rags came to me and made me shiver.

As my eyes adjusted to the dimness, I saw that the room had a single window, but it was shuttered, allowing in only slits of grey light. The floorboards were bowed and rotting in places, and the roof— invisible in the darkness—was held up by gnarled posts.

"Arthur, get them some decent clothes," Lovell shouted as he slumped into a chair next to the table. Then he pointed at Robert, Alfred and the other two boys. "Bring me your takings."

While Lovell shouted at the boys for their insufficient earnings, Arthur led us to a pile of musty clothes and had us pick through it looking for

35

something that fit. We each found a pair of pants and long shirts and, at Arthur's insistence, took off our own clothes and put them on. Then we found some worn leather shoes and exchanged them for our Nikes. Felt hats completed our outfits.

"You don't look quite so odd now," Arthur observed. "You just look like scarecrows."

"You," Lovell shouted. I looked and saw he was pointing at me. "Bring me your clothes, and your bags."

"Yes, sir," I said.

"Ha, nice manners," Lovell said. "Now bring them here."

With a sinking feeling, I brought our bundles—including our cloak—along with our clothing, to Lovell. He opened Nicholas's bundle and rifled through the few belongings we had, then he inspected our clothes.

"What manner of cloth is this?" he asked. "I have never seen the like."

I didn't think he was expecting an answer, but then he glared at me. "Well? Where did you get them? Did you steal them?"

"No," I said. "They're ours. Our parents bought them for us."

He looked at me through narrowed eyes. "Are they rich."

I glanced around the room. "Richer than you, I'd guess,"

Lovell slammed the sneaker he had been inspecting against the table, making me jump. "I may not look like much," he said, "but I can still whip the tar out of you, so watch your tongue, boy. Now, where did you get these?"

"Wynantskill," I said. "That's where we're from."

Lovell shook his head. "I have heard of no such place. Do you seek to fool me, boy?"

"No. It's in the south. Near Horsham."

He put the sneaker down and reached for the cloak. "That I have heard of. Were you in jail there?"

"Never," I said.

Lovell grunted. "I don't suppose it would matter if you were." He pulled open my bundle and held up the cloak. "And what is this."

"Our cloak," I said. "Our grandfather gave it to us."

Lovell stood and threw the cloak around his shoulders. "You trifle with me, boy. No one is going to give you something this fine. Look at you, a beggar, nothing more."

"But you dressed us like this. And that's ours."

I thought he might hit me, but instead he smirked. "It is mine now. Everything you own, everything you earn, belongs to me. But do not look so glum. This will feed you for a week, until you learn to properly pay your own way. And these …" He bent and scooped up our clothes, "… these will bring a fine price."

He put our clothes and shoes in a box under his table, fastened the cloak around his neck and dismissed me with a wave of his hand.

I went back to where Nicolas, Charlie and Arthur waited, with my shoulders slumped.

"We've lost our clothes, and the cloak."

Charlie shook his head. "Again."

Arthur clapped a hand on my shoulder. "You've done well to gain Lovell's favour. This will buy you some time. Make use of it."

He led us to a far corner of the room. "You'll sleep here." We looked down. There were a few tattered blankets lying on the warped floorboards. "And you will eat here and stay here when you are not at work."

"What do we do now?" Nicholas asked.

"Your day will start early and run late. If I were you, I would take the opportunity to rest. The others will be back soon. And after our meal, it will be time to practice."

"Practice what?" Charlie asked as Arthur walked away.

"You will see," he said without turning.

SCENE V

A Lodging House in London

CHARLIE

I was angry about losing our cloak (again) but also worried about Lovell taking our clothes. What if we managed to get our cloak back and went home wearing our medieval out fits? Would we return naked? And what would happen to our 21st century clothes? What would the 14th century make of our Nike sneakers? But then I figured there were more pressing things to worry about, though I didn't expect one of them to be Nicholas. Me and Mitch were discouraged, but Nicholas appeared heartbroken.

His bottom lip began quivering, his eyes grew moist, and then he slumped down next to the wall, put his hands over his face, and started crying. We both stared at him, embarrassed and worried that the others would notice. I sat down next to him and put an arm around his shoulder.

"It's all right," I said. "We'll figure something out."

Nicolas sniffed and wiped his nose with his sleeve. His eyes were puffy and red. "No, it is not all right," he said, grinding at his tears with the heels of his palms. "This is a disaster."

"Look, I know this isn't great," I said, keeping my voice low, hoping Nicholas would do the same, "but we've been in worse places."

Mitch knelt in front of us, shielding Nicholas from view. "Charlie's right. We've got a place to stay, and you'll get to perform on the streets of London, which is what you wanted to do."

Nicolas gaped at him in disbelief. "You really don't understand what's happening, do you?"

Mitch and I looked at one another and shrugged.

"We're being forced to join a guild," I said. "Yeah, it's not ideal, but it might be better than going freelance."

"This is a gang of thieves," Nicolas hissed. "We're being recruited to steal, and if we don't steal, we'll be beaten and thrown onto the streets to beg, and if we do, we could be hanged."

I didn't know about Mitch, but now I felt like crying.

"We have to find a way to escape," Nicolas said, taking a deep breath. "So, the most important thing right now is to make them believe we want to stay."

"That'll be easier if you stop crying," I whispered.

Nicolas nodded and, seeing that he wasn't going to start blubbering again, I removed my arm.

"We will need to be cooperative," he said, "do as they say, pretend we want to be part of their gang. If we convince them, they may drop their guard, and that will give us a chance to escape."

Mitch nodded. "But we're not leaving without our cloak."

"We may have to," Nicolas said. "You are never going to get it back, and we should take the first opportunity that comes our way." He looked to me for support, but I shook my head.

"We must have the cloak. Without it, we're

trapped."

Nicholas's brow furrowed. He looked from me to Mitch and back again and seemed to be about to speak when we heard a rapping sound. Lovell heaved himself out of his chair and shuffled to the door, where he flicked open the peek hole and undid the latch. Another group of boys came in, smaller and younger than we were, but dressed in the same ragged clothing. Back at the table, they handed Lovell their coins as he berated them for not having made enough and cuffed a few of them on the ear. After taking his abuse, they sat near the far wall, glancing occasionally in our direction.

Other groups came in after that—different boys, some older, some younger—but the ritual was always the same: a coded knock brought Lovell to the door, then he would relieve them of their money, knock some heads, and wait for the next group. The boys clustered together in groups and generally stayed away from us, but some came over to slap us on the back and call us "fresh meat," always with big grins on their faces.

"We're fresh," Nicolas said, once we were alone again. "We have never been caught stealing before. If one of the older boys gets nicked, we'll be the ones in the dock. It will go easier on us the first time and Lovell will get to keep his more experienced gang members."

"What will happen to us?" Mitch asked.

"We'll be branded, or whipped, or both," Nicolas said. "And then Lovell will be there to take us back when we're released. I tell you, we are trapped here, and we're heading for the gallows."

"What can we do?" I asked, trying to keep the panic out of my voice.

41

"The only thing we can," Nicholas said. "Gain their trust, learn their trade, and make sure we don't get caught."

When the room was practically filled with restless boys, and the light leaking through the shutters disappeared, Lovell lit a few lanterns. The babble of voices grew loud, but Lovell continued to sit at his table, counting coins and writing in a ledger. Then someone knocked and the room went quiet, and the boys began moving forward as Lovell went to open the door. Two skinny men entered, one carrying several bulging sacks and the other a large, covered pot. The boys eyed them in anticipation.

The men waited while Lovell counted out a few coins and placed them into the outstretched hand of the man who had carried in the sacks. He looked at the coins and put them in a purse hanging from his belt. Then he picked up one of the sacks and dumped a load of bread onto the floor. It wasn't full loaves, just big hunks, and the thudding it made as it hit the boards confirmed that it was also stale. But the boys dove on it and the room exploded into shouts and crying and thumping as the boys fought one another for each piece.

Then the other man took the lid off the pot and began ladling something into wooden bowls he took from another sack. The boys lurched toward him, but Lovell and the men cuffed and pushed and shouted until they formed a disorderly line that became more and more disorderly the further back it went.

"That must be dinner," Nicholas said. "We'd better join them or we'll go hungry."

As it turned out, we went hungry anyway. A few of the boys were still scuffling over the last of the bread when we got there, and the boys at the front of the line had already claimed their bowls of thin stew or soup or whatever it was and had scuttled off into darkened corners to eat. We were the last ones served, and by then there was no bread left and only a ladleful of broth. The man scooped it into a single bowl, and we returned to our blankets and shared it.

One of the boys collected the bowls. He came to us first, smiling as he pulled it out of Mitch's hands before he could gulp down the final drops. After the men took the bowls, bags, and pot away, Lovell lit a few more lanterns and called the boys into the centre of the big room. "Come on, ye little skivers," he yelled. "Practice time. And the best boy gets a treat."

The boys cheered and crowded into the open area. We followed, standing on the outskirts of the group.

"Arthur, Alfred," Lovell said. "Show the new boys how it's done."

Arthur and Alfred came to us as the crowd of boys broke up into teams and began working at their particular talent. Soon the room was filled with juggling, jumping, and stilt-walking boys, and another group that seemed to be milling around doing nothing.

"You two with us," Arthur said, grabbing me and Nicolas by the arms. "We'll show you a few tricks."

"What about me?" Mitch asked.

Alfred pointed to the centre of the room. "Go see Lovell," he said.

SCENE VI

A Lodging House in London

MITCH

I walked toward the middle of the room, feeling suddenly alone. Activity swirled all around me and at the centre was Lovell, still wearing our cloak. He didn't seem to be waiting for me or watching for me and I thought for a moment that I might duck into a dark corner and hide, but I knew that would be futile.

Charlie and Nicolas were with Arthur and Alfred learning, I supposed, some better acrobatics. I suddenly envied them. At least they were together. I didn't know what Lovell had in store for me, but I was pretty sure I wasn't going to like it.

Lovell still had his back to me as I approached and the thought of ripping the cloak off him came, unbidden, to my mind. I put it away even before he turned around and glared at me. It would be as stupid as trying to hide in a corner. Stupider, even. And I understood, as Nicholas insisted, that our best chance of getting away was to pretend we didn't want to.

"Your friends have some talent," Lovell said, raising his head to make eye contact. Charlie and I weren't the tallest kids in the room, but we were taller than most, and that included Lovell. He pointed with his chin toward where Arthur was showing Nicholas how to do a double flip, and Charlie, under Alfred's guidance, was learning to juggle. "You, I am told, do not share their aptitude for the performance arts. Is this so?"

"I have different talents," I said. "I can read and write."

Lovell scoffed. "So can I, boy. Your education won't put bread in your compatriot's mouths. Look around you: the welfare of those boys, and yourself, depends on you pulling lour, and scribes do not—"

"I made enough money on—"

A quick slap to the side of my head cut me off.

"This is London, boy. People with your fine ways are ten a penny. The carls in the countryside might have been impressed with your knowledge, but here you won't earn enough groats to buy a decent meal. You need to learn a new skill if you want to survive."

"Okay," I said, rubbing the side of my face. "What sort of skill?"

Lovell pointed to a plump, curly haired boy. "Dobbs," he barked, "Show this boy how to draw. See that he learns well."

Dobbs came to us. He stared at me through narrowed eyes. "You the one they call the scribe?"

I nodded.

"He is no scribe while he is with us," Lovell said. "His education counts for nothing."

Dobbs pointed over his shoulder with his thumb. "This way Not-a-Scribe."

"It's Mitch," I said.

I saw Lovell's hand move and flinched in preparation for another cuff on the ear, but he merely placed his hand on my shoulder and asked in a quiet voice. "Tell me, boy, where did you get your education?"

I looked him in the eye. "The same place where my grandfather gave me that cloak you're wearing. The same land where I live with my family, in a house bigger than you'll ever see. A kingdom called Wynantskill."

I wanted to intimidate him, or at least impress him. I failed on both counts. Lovell laughed and slapped my shoulder, nearly knocking me sideways. "Well, that is no kingdom I have heard of, and it means nothing to me, to you, or the Queen's Guards. So, learn well from Dobbs, unless you want to write epitaphs for the starving urchins that line our alleyways."

Dobbs led me away to where a group of boys was walking around, doing nothing.

"I'm not very good at drawing, either," I said, trotting after him. "I only got a C in art class."

Dobbs turned to me. "What are you talking about?"

"Drawing," I said. "Making picture with a pencil or pen."

Dobbs smiled and shook his head. "It is not that sort of drawing. This is what you need to do." He placed a small stone in my hand. "Put that in your pocket." I did. Then he handed me a handkerchief. "Now put that in your other pocket."

"Okay, now what?"

Dobbs looked at me, his brow furrowed. "What do you mean by 'Okay'?"

I thought for a moment. "It means 'all right,' or 'everything's fine,' or 'I understand'."

"All of those things? All at once."

I nodded. "It's a versatile word."

"It is strange. Did you learn it in your kingdom of Wynantskill?"

"Yes, along with many other things."

"And you lived in a big house? And your grandfather was rich, and powerful?"

"Rich and powerful enough," I said.

Dobbs nodded slowly. "Okay," he said, grinning. "But your grandfather is not here, and you are no longer living in your grand house, so you still need to learn how to draw."

"How?"

The group of boys were now wandering around us. Dobbs watched them as they walked by. "Everyone here has the same items in their pockets—a stone, which represents a coin, and a handkerchief. The object is, to be the boy with the most stones and handkerchiefs."

I looked at the boys, then back at Dobbs. "What am I supposed to do?"

As a boy walked near, Dobbs reached out and drew his hand back with a stone in it. "It only counts if they don't notice," he said, watching the boy continue on his way. Instinctively, I felt my own pockets. The stone and the handkerchief were gone.

Dobbs laughed. "I guess you need more basic instruction." He grabbed another boy and pulled him aside. "Here," he said, stuffing a handkerchief into the boy's back pocket. "Try it when he's standing still."

I reached toward the boy, my hand shaking. There was no way I was going to be able to get near it. The boy's shirt hung down over his pants and I couldn't even see his pocket. Dobbs laughed again. "You have not a clue, do you?" His hand flashed toward the boy and returned with the handkerchief.

"Can I try that?" said a voice from behind me. I turned and saw it was Nicolas. He looked at Dobbs. "I would like to learn."

"Well," Dobbs said. "This one here is not much of a student. Let's see what you can do."

After that, it went easier. I watched Nicolas, who wasn't afraid to try, and followed his lead. He failed, time and again, but he kept trying, and that gave me the confidence to try, and fail, myself. We worked with Dobbs for the rest of the evening, and after a few hours I found I could draw out a stone or handkerchief—on occasion—without the mark noticing. I was nowhere near as good as Nicholas, however, who seemed to have a natural talent.

It started to annoy me that he and Charlie were so good at things, but then I looked to where Alfred was teaching Charlie some juggling tricks, and Charlie was dropping more clubs than he caught, so I didn't feel quite so bad.

We practiced late into the night, and fell onto our blankets tired and sore and, in Charlie's case, not at all happy about being abandoned. He seemed to have forgotten that I had been the one who had originally been abandoned and looked at Nicholas accusingly.

"What were you playing at?" he asked petulantly and, I noted, with a hint of London dialect. "You left me alone with that slave-driver, Alfred."

Nicholas sat next to him and laid a hand on his thigh. "Listen," he said, in a voice that drained the anger from Charlie's face, "if we're going to survive here, we need to learn everything we can. We must blend in and become one of them. Otherwise, we will never escape."

Charlie nodded and laid down. Nicholas laid next to him. I pulled the blanket over the three of us, lying next to Charlie.

"But we're not leaving without our cloak," I said.

SCENE VII

A Lodging House in London

CHARLIE

It was impossible to keep up with everything Alfred and Arthur wanted to teach me. I didn't mind being a bad student. I didn't even mind that Nicolas was better than me. But I did mind that he was so much better. He already knew how to do acrobatics, but then he learned to juggle and pick pockets. All I could do were the few, simple flips, and Mitch couldn't even do that. Compared to the other boys, we looked hopeless, which made Nicolas nervous.

"You must try harder," he told me during our third practice session. "You do not want to be the least capable."

He said this while I was tossing bean bags (easier to catch than juggling clubs) into the air, and occasionally catching them, so I tried to impress him by juggling them, but kept moving forward to catch them, which was a rookie mistake.

"Then why don't you try to be less capable," I said, as I totally lost control and dropped all three bags. "Then we wouldn't look so bad."

Nicolas shook his head, gathered up the bags and pulled me to the edge of the room. "Stand in front of the wall when you juggle, then you won't be able to

49

keep lurching forward."

"That's nuts," I said, as he threw the bags to me.

"Just try it."

"What makes you so …," I started juggling, and kept juggling.

"Practice like that until you're confident, then try it away from the wall, and then try the clubs."

I nodded, amazed I was keeping all three bags in the air.

"You need to be better," he said, stepping close. "Lovell is watching you and your brother. He may decide you are not worth investing in. If he turns you or your brother out, I do not know how we will find each other again."

I caught the bean bags—one, two, three—and turned to him. "That's easy for you to say. We've never done anything like this before. And you practice like your life depends on it."

He leaned closer. "It does. Now try juggling four."

I looked down as he laid a stone on top of the bags. With my free hand, I felt my pocket. It was empty. "Cut that out!"

Nicolas smiled and turned away. "Be better," he said.

After that, I took my training a little more seriously, and so did Mitch, though it didn't do him a lot of good. I soon got better at juggling, and even graduated to the clubs, which pleased Alfred, but Mitch could only juggle the bean bags and do a few simple flips. He did pretty well on the stilts, however, but not well enough to be a performer, so mostly he acted as a lookout.

We might have had a roof over our heads and food every day, but it wasn't an easy life. We were up before dawn, shoved onto the streets in all weathers, and not allowed to return until dark. And if we didn't return with enough coins, we would get a clout from Mr. Lovell. We slept on the floor, the food was awful, the room smelled, and there was always a brawl or something going on that kept us from getting enough sleep.

The bathroom, which they called the 'privy' or 'jakes,' was in the back alley and … well, I won't tell you how awful it was, I'll just tell you that me and Mitch preferred the trench latrines we used in the army. They were cleaner, and they smelled better. None of us wanted to be there, but every time Nicolas talked about escaping, all I could see were the filthy faces of the children, dressed in rags, huddled in the streets.

While we were out, Nicolas ignored the beggars and the drunks, but it was harder for us. We couldn't believe the state they were in, or why no one would help them. We would have, if we could, but we were having a hard enough time surviving on our own. I guess everyone else was in the same boat, and as bad as our boat was, at least we had a place to sleep and the promise of an occasional meal.

And so, we spent our evenings juggling, stilt walking and learning acrobatics from Arthur and Alfred, desperate to remain useful so we'd have a place to stay, and—as Mitch kept reminding us—so we could be near the cloak. In a few days, I began to improve, and Nicolas, who had started out good, became amazing.

Mitch never caught up with us, but he was good enough to be included in some of the big stunts where he didn't have to perform, like the one we worked out where we would launch Nicolas into the air so he could do astounding flips and spins—a trick that even impressed Arthur.

They didn't let us steal because they knew we'd get caught and that wouldn't be good for 'business.' That was fine with us. We just did the performing and, when a suitably large crowd had gathered, the other boys would mingle among them, picking what they could.

Sometimes a few of them would get chased, and once one of them was caught, which caused some concern. With no criminal record, one of us might be substituted for him so we could take his punishment, but it turned out it was the first time he'd been nicked, so they let him off with just a whipping.

The other boys weren't exactly good to us, but they mostly left us alone. Early on, a few of them had started bullying Nicolas, but me and Mitch stood up to them and they soon backed down. A rumour that we were from a wealthy family started going around and, with each circuit, the story grew until we were given a sort of grudging respect, meaning they stayed even further away from us.

Arthur and Alfred were the closest we had to friends, but they let us know they were only teaching us because it made their lives easier. For our part, we did what we were told: we practiced, performed, and tried to make them believe we were happy to stay there.

After a week or so, Nicolas told us he had an idea about how we might escape, but Mitch told him we weren't leaving without the cloak.

"You are content to remain a prisoner here?" Nicolas asked him. "Do I need to remind you we are living on borrowed time?"

"Do I need to remind you," Mitch replied, "that without the cloak, we can't get home?"

We were sitting in our usual spot, on our tattered blankets, after a tiring day spent performing on the streets, fighting for food, and practicing.

"And do I need to remind you that a hangman's noose waits for us? If the boy who was caught had been known to the guards, one of us would be in prison now."

"We have to take that chance. We have no choice. We need the cloak."

Nicolas threw his hands in the air and turned to me. "Are you willing to risk swinging from the gallows waiting for an opportunity that will never come?"

I looked from Nicolas to Mitch and back again. "I'm sorry," I said, wondering why I was apologizing, "but we need the cloak."

Nicolas grabbed one of the blankets and began stomping away.

"Hey," I said, grabbing his arm. "Where do you think you're going?"

"Away from you," he said, his lip trembling. I was afraid he might start crying, but he was more angry than frustrated. "You may be content to die, but I am not."

The room, up until then a babble of voices, grew quiet as Lovell doused the lanterns.

"Keep your voice down," I said. "And come back."

"No!"

"Lover's tiff," someone said. A few of the boys giggled.

I tried to pull him back, but he resisted. "You're attracting attention. Now come on."

He gave in and threw his blanket down near where we slept. When I laid down next to him, he moved away and turned his back to me. On my other side, Mitch had also turned away. I laid in the darkness, listening to silence descend, wondering how I had got in the middle, between Nicolas and Mitch. Or was it Nicolas getting between Mitch and me?

I never found the answer because a sudden pounding broke the stillness.

In the dim light of Lovell's candle, I saw the boys raise their heads, look around, then pretend to go back to sleep. Mitch and Nicolas woke, as well. All three of us looked to the door, worried that we were being raided. Lovell, still counting coins at his table, jumped from his seat, holding his hand over his heart. When the pounding came again, he lit a second candle and crept to the door. When the pounding stopped again, he looked through the little window, then stepped back and opened the door.

Light flooded the dark room as two men with torches entered. They were followed by a tall, skinny man wearing a velvet jerkin, silk tights and leather buskins. I knew about these things because the gang always pointed them out to us when we were in the streets. They were the mark of wealthy people, and wealthy people were good for business. The man strutted into the room, and, to our surprise, Lovell bowed to him. "Lord Fordyn," Lovell said. "You honour me."

Fordyn pushed Lovell aside and strode across the room, his torch bearers following. "And you cheat me." He and his men went to the table where Lovell's ledger and the strongbox were. "You have cut your pledge short. Fulfil your obligation now."

Lovell scurried toward him, his head bowed. "Sir, I beg you, the takings have been lower than expected."

Fordyn nodded to one of his torch bearers. "Cuthbert, I believe this man is lying."

"No," Lovell said. "I swear, I have given all—"

Cuthbert struck Lovell, sending him sprawling on the floorboards. Fordyn nodded to the other man. "Edmond, convince our friend that he has more to give." As Edmond approached the cowering Lovell, I noticed all the other boys were asleep, or pretending to be.

"We should not be too curious about this," Nicolas, who was suddenly by my side, said. "Lay down. Sleep."

I tried, but it was impossible to sleep with all the shouting and begging going on, and harder still to not peek at what was happening.

I had thought that Lovell was imposing, but Edmond, with his broad shoulders and sturdy arms, had Lovell weeping on the floorboards.

"It will be paid, I swear," Lovell said, holding his arms over his head to ward off another blow. "I just need more time. You know how it is during times of troubles, people grasp onto their purses, they are less generous."

"And that is precisely why you need to pay. Now!" Fordyn said.

Cuthbert moved in, taking over where Edmond left off. He raised his hand and Lovell covered his head. When Cuthbert saw he couldn't hit him, he kicked him, instead. Lovell groaned and crawled backward, under his table.

"The Armada was spied off the coast of Cornwall yesterday," Fordyn continued. "The Spanish will not wait, and neither can I."

"The money," Lovell said, "all of it, is in the box. That's all there is."

Fordyn opened the box and quickly counted the money, pocketing it as he did. I heard a few low moans nearby. There would be no breakfast in the morning.

Fordyn turned the box over, checking for a false bottom. Then he threw it to the floor. "This is half what you owe," he bellowed, kicking at Lovell who continued to cower under the table. "I will leave here satisfied, or I will carve out an ounce of your flesh for every pound you owe me."

Lovell let out a squeak. Then I heard him groping around under the table. In a few moments, he crawled out, holding our cloak. I shook Nicolas and Mitch.

"Look," I whispered.

Lovell held the cloak up for Fordyn to see. "Here, take this, just do not harm me."

Fordyn looked at the cloak, took it from Lovell, and stroked it. "Where did you get this?" he asked, his voice hushed.

Lovell stared up at him. "What does it matter? One of my boys stole it."

Fordyn gazed around the room at the sleeping boys. "Which one? I should like to know who he stole it from."

"The boy," Lovell stammered. "He came to me some time ago. I took the cloak as payment for his board. He ... he didn't work out. I sent him back to the streets."

Fordyn turned his gaze back on Lovell. "Is that so?"

"On my life. Will you take the cloak as payment?"

Fordyn shook his head. "Half payment. But this will satisfy me for the moment."

"Thank you, thank you," Lovell said, still on his knees. Fordyn draped the cloak around his shoulders and fastened it. "I will return in a fortnight. You will have the rest of my money, plus interest, then. Or I will have your life."

Without a word, Fordyn turned and strode from the

room, followed by Cuthbert and Edmond. As they disappeared through the door, darkness returned.

"Well," Nicolas whispered in the silence. "Do you want to escape now?"

SCENE VIII

A London street

MITCH

We were all eager to get away after that, but even with us all in agreement, we found that escaping wasn't going to be easy. Nicolas told us he had a plan, but that it wasn't ready yet. We asked him what it was, but he wouldn't tell us. Not even Charlie could get it out of him.

In the days that followed, Nicolas practiced picking pockets every chance he got. He practiced on back pockets, front pockets, vest pockets and coat pockets. He practised picking pockets while standing still, walking, and even running past the mark. We practised too. It was a requirement, but neither of us showed much promise. Nicolas, however, became so skilled at pulling a wallet out of a pocket that Lovell began considering him for the second team. But, despite his new talent, Nicolas still wanted to be a performer.

As performers, our job was merely to draw a crowd. We kept them amused while the second team mingled among them, taking what they could. We told ourselves that, as long as we only performed, we weren't really thieves, but Nicolas assured us the law would not look at it that way, and it was only a matter of time before we were nicked.

Nicolas came up with a plan for that too. If one of us was grabbed, the captive was to shout "Break," and that would alert the other two. They would run in opposite directions to confuse any pursuers and one or both of them would circle around behind the scuffle and drop down on his hands and knees. All the captive had to do then was push his captor backward to trip him.

We practiced it with the help of some of the other boys. It did work, as long as everyone did as they were supposed to, even the guy capturing us, and as long as only one of us was being nicked. The other boys thought it was a waste of time, but Nicolas kept us practicing it until they refused to help us anymore. We just hoped his escape plan was better.

When he wasn't performing, or practicing picking pockets, or working on our acrobat routine with Arthur and Alfred, Nicolas had us helping him with his high flip. It was an impressive trick, but it required all three of us and Nicolas would sulk if I said I wanted to get some sleep instead. I didn't see the use in practicing it, we were already tossing Nicolas up as high as we could, but he kept telling us we could do better.

The only good thing was, now that the cloak was out of reach, we were all obsessed with getting away, which kept Nicolas and Charlie from bickering. Every day—as we performed, practiced, or lay in bed at night—we remained alert, looking for any chance to escape, but even though we were starting to be regarded as part of the gang, we still weren't trusted. If we edged away from the group, two or three of the older boys would suddenly appear by our sides, glaring at us until we moved back. This meant we had to balance between pretending to be part of the gang, and

59

constantly being on the lookout for a chance to run (while not being obvious about it), all the while worrying that someone might get nicked, which would see one or all of us in jail. It was exhausting.

Then, one morning as we trudged through the streets looking for a likely place to draw a crowd, Nicolas told us it was time.

"It has been raining for three days. Today we see the sun for the first time in a week. People will be out in great number, and they will be glad for entertainment."

"But Arthur and Alfred will still be watching us," I said.

Nicolas nodded. "All we need is a distraction. Wait, and watch."

True to his prediction, the crowd that morning was larger than we had seen in a long time. Charlie and Nicolas performed their routines. I helped when I could and kept watch for the guards when I couldn't. The boys began to circulate among the crowd. No one noticed. It was going to be a profitable day for Lovell.

Then a man riding a horse paused to watch us, a gentleman, well-dressed in fine clothes and a long coat. Nicolas, taking advantage of a short break, pulled me and Charlie close. "This is our chance," he whispered. "Be ready."

Before Arthur and Alfred could begin the next routine, Nicolas called to the man on the horse. "Sir, would you like to see a feat never before attempted?" Arthur and Alfred looked on suspiciously, but Nicolas continued. "For a ha'penny, I will jump over you and your horse."

The man looked down, amused. "For such a slender lad as yourself, that would surely be impossible." But he pulled his coin purse from his breast pocket and looked into it. "You have, however, piqued my curiosity and, as it happens, I have a ha'penny to spare. I will gladly give it if you live up to your promise." He returned the purse to his pocket and patted his coat. "And I won't have to worry that you are out to pick my pocket," he laughed, "as you are down there, and I am up here."

Nicolas beamed. "Who wishes to see me jump over this man and his horse?" he asked, turning to the street traffic. Soon, an even larger crowd gathered, and the pick pockets eagerly mingled among them.

"Do our trick," Nicolas whispered to us, "and follow my lead."

The three of us walked to the horse. We went to the far side so Nicolas could land closer to the crowd. None of the boys followed; they seemed as eager to see our trick as the crowd was. Nicolas nodded to us and stepped back a few yards, then he ran forward, jumped into our clasped hands and we launched him into the air as far as we could. The crowd gasped as Nicolas flipped—his head nearly touching the man's head— and landed on the other side of the horse.

The crowd applauded and cheered, even Arthur and Alfred. Nicolas grinned. "My ha'penny, sir?"

The man reached into his breast pocket. "You have fulfilled your end of the bargain," he said. Then his face turned to one of confusion. "My purse, it's—"

"Nothing to fear, sir," Nicolas said, extending his hand with the purse in it. The man's expression changed from confusion, to anger, to gratitude. He leaned down and snatched it from Nicolas, letting out a nervous laugh as he looked inside. "All here," he said. "That was a worthy trick." He pulled a ha'penny out and tossed it to Nicolas.

"Always a good idea to keep a hand on your coin purse," Nicolas said.

The man chuckled nervously, as did many people in the crowd. Then the man tucked it away and patted his pocket, which prompted others to do the same. Almost instantly, a cry went up from the crowd.

"My purse, it's gone!"

"Mine too!"

"My handkerchief!"

"You, boy! Stop thief!"

"There's another one. Get him."

The gang ducked and dodged as the crowd pressed in on them. Arthur, Alfred, and the others scattered. Nicolas ran around the horse and shot past us. "Come on," he shouted.

We ran after him, into the maze of crowded streets. Behind us, we heard Arthur calling to the others. "After them, they're getting away."

Dodging horses and pushing through throngs of people, we bolted down the street, then turned and raced, single file, down a narrow alley, splashing through puddles of foul-smelling water. We hoped that would be enough to throw them off, but as we exited the alley, the sound of shouts and splashing followed us. The street we found ourselves on was narrow and practically deserted.

"This is bad" Charlie said, "we need a crowd to blend into."

We ran to a junction and stopped, searching for a more crowded street.

"This way," Nicolas said.

"But there's more people over there," I said, following.

"And that is the way they will go," Nicolas said. "I hope."

Midway down the lane, we dodged into another alley and came out onto a street of more dilapidated houses. Behind us, we heard the shouts of our pursuers.

"They are not going to give up," Nicolas said. "We need to get off the streets."

We ran further, to where a large wooden building sat at the corner of two narrow lanes. It appeared deserted, and was unlocked, so we scurried inside, slamming the door behind us.

We found ourselves in a cavernous space, lit by large, open windows high above the floor. The room was silent, but not empty. Standing on a raised platform in the middle of the floor, a cluster of four startled men stared in our direction. They were dressed strangely, in garish clothes and hats, and all clutched papers in their hands. They had been talking when we entered, but now they were silent.

One of them, a tall, skinny man in a comically ornate outfit of tight pants and a long, gold-edged coat, turned toward us. "You, boys, who are you, and what mischief are you up to?"

Nicolas rushed forward, and we followed. Two of the men drew daggers.

"Good sirs," he said, panting. "My name is Nicolas Fen. My friends and I are in peril. Criminals are after us. They took us into their gang, but we have escaped. Show us mercy, I beg you, our pursuers will be upon us in moments."

A young man with a thin moustache and dark hair stepped forward. Like the others, he was dressed strangely—red leggings, blue jerkin, gaudy cape—but was not holding any papers. He spread his arms wide and, although looking at us, spoke as if he was addressing a crowd. "And you wish us to accept that you are of sound character?"

"We are, sir," Nicolas said.

The skinny man pointed his dagger at us. "So you say."

The young man nodded slowly. "What are we to make of this? The surest way to discern a thief is to let him show himself what he is and steal out of our company."

The skinny man stepped up next to him, still pointing his dagger. "Then best to send them on their way before they do."

"We are not thieves," Nicolas said, his voice rising. "We were taken against our will. We have merely been performers, none of us have taken anything that does not belong to us. We are straight-fingered, and true."

"Performers," the younger man said, grinning. "Splendid!" He clapped his hands together. The sound echoed through the room. "Costumes," he shouted.

Scattered around the raised platform were several large trunks. These were opened, garments were pulled out and one of them was shoved over my head, followed by a hat. Within seconds, all three of us were dressed in loose outfits of coarse, murrey-coloured material. Then empty ale mugs were thrust into our hands. The men pulled us onto the platform and, still holding their sheets of paper, spread around us to keep us hidden. We tried our best to stop gasping for breath and calm ourselves so we looked natural and not scared to death.

"You are in a tavern," the young man said. "Pretend to drink. You are having a good time." Then he turned to the rest of the men. "Shall we begin where we left off?"

The skinny man cleared his throat and turned to one of the others—an old man in a tatty, hooded cloak—and, glancing at his papers, began speaking. "How, Harry, whence come you?"

The old man, without looking at his paper, spoke. "My noble lord, from Eastcheap."

"The complaints I hear of thee are grievous."

"Nay," the old man said. "They are false."

"Swear you, ungracious boy? Thou are violently carried away from grace and the devil hunts thee in the likeness of an old man."

"Whom means your grace?"

"A villainous misleader of youth, a white-bearded Satan. You must banish him from your life, nay, from this kingdom, from life itself."

"I know that man, my lord, but I know more harm in myself than in he. That he is old, more the pity, but to say he is evil, I utterly deny."

The old man stopped speaking for a moment and pulled his cloak back, revealing a head of shaggy grey hair and a long beard. He looked directly at me, and I saw the scar, running up his cheek and curling around his right eye like a question mark. "Banish me," he said, "and you banish all the earth."

I didn't think I could be any more frightened, but my stomach turned to ice and dropped to the floor. It was the druid, and that meant the danger we were in was about to get much worse.

Then Arthur and three other boys pounded in through the door. The young man with the moustache looked at them and smiled. "A well-timed entrance. You would be Bardolph, with a message from the sheriff?"

The boys stopped. "Sheriff?" Arthur asked. "What are you on about?"

"We are an acting company, and you have entered our play. Do you wish to join?"

"When pigs fly," Arthur said, as the others fanned out beside him.

"Ah, well, if you do not wish to be a player, perhaps you have come to enjoy our performance. I fear we are not going on until this evening, but do return, and bring your penny for the gate."

Arthur shook his head and scanned the room. Then he looked back at the man. "Daft bugger," he said. "Come on lads, they may not be here, but they are surely close by."

They ran back into the street. In moments, the sound of their footfalls faded, and silence returned.

"Thank you, sir," Nicolas said, but I barely heard him. I was staring at the old man. When Charlie saw me, he stared too.

"And what can you offer us in return for your rescue?" the young man asked.

Nicolas pulled the quill from my pocket. "This," he said. Then he waved a hand toward me and Charlie. "They are scholars, they can read and write. You have need of that?" Then he bowed. "And I am an actor."

The man laughed. "If you have half as much talent as brass, you will be the best actor in London. And you," he said to me and Charlie, "are you truly scribes?"

I nodded, still looking at the old man who was now ambling toward us. "Yes," I said. "We read and write. Both of us."

The old man stopped in front of me and Charlie, his blue eyes twinkling. "Hell-o Mitch, hell-o Charlie," he said. "I have been expecting you."

Nicolas and the young man looked at us, open-mouthed.

"You know them, Mendel?" the young man asked.

The old man nodded. "I do."

"And you can vouch for their character?"

"I can, and I will. They are brave and loyal and there is nothing false about them."

"Then I am glad to have you in our troupe," the young man said, slapping Nicolas on the back. "I trust you will find the company of actors more agreeable than a den of thieves, even if only marginally."

The men, with the exception of Mendel, laughed. Charlie looked at Nicolas and shrugged.

"Actors," Nicolas said, "are looked upon as little better than thieves."

"Right you are, young Nicholas," the man said. "But rest assured your necks are safer with us."

He slapped Nicolas on the back again, then made a mock bow. "Welcome, my young friends," he said. "I am pleased to make your acquaintance. My name is William Shakespeare."

ACT II

SCENE I

A Playhouse in London

CHARLIE

We weren't sure if we were more surprised to be with William Shakespeare or with Malcolm, who now called himself Mendel. Mitch leaned over and whispered that we shouldn't let on that we knew who Mr. Shakespeare was, on account of him being so famous and all, as that might raise questions and draw unwanted attention. I agreed with that, but we had to acknowledge that we knew Mendel, because he had said we did.

Although that satisfied Mr. Shakespeare—or William, as he preferred us to call him—it didn't satisfy me. How did he get here, why was he expecting us, and what were we doing here? Those, and a hundred other questions zipped around inside my head, but Mendel merely stepped back into his original position without a word. The other two men—Franklin and Godwin—stripped the costumes off us, put them away and returned to their papers, leaving William standing nearby, watching us as he thoughtfully stroked his chin.

"And what are we to do with you," he said quietly, as if musing to himself.

"They'll bring trouble," Franklin, the tall, skinny

one who had pointed a dagger at us, said.

Godwin, shorter, darker, and broader, nodded. "Ramsey will not be best pleased."

William continued looking at us as he waved a hand in their direction. "Leave Ramsey to me. These boys came to us for help, and we cannot turn them away. And I am certain they can find ways to make themselves useful."

"We could act," Nicolas said, his face beaming with excitement. "Or do tricks for the audience."

William laughed. "I fear we haven't time to test your talents. It may yet be early, but after my friends, very kindly, help me with my play, we need to practice hard for tonight's performance. While we work, you will need to make yourselves useful in a more mundane, but no less important, manner."

The excitement drained from Nicolas's face. I looked at him, confused. "He means muck out the stalls," he said. Franklin and Godwin, laughed.

William, meanwhile, ran off and returned with two brooms and a rake. "Here," he said, handing them to us. "The floorboards around the stage, and the floor near the entrance, they all need to be swept clear. After that, if you do a good job, you can help set up for this evening's performance. And don't be such a gloomy-guts," he continued, looking at Nicolas. "The life of a thespian is not all glamor. Your chance will come in time, but right now, it's all hands to the pump. Work hard, be useful, and perhaps Ramsey will not throw you back into the street."

That was all Nicolas needed. He immediately took charge, leading us around the room and showing us what to do. The brooms weren't like the brooms Mom uses, they were more like the ones witches ride on in

Halloween cartoons, so it was difficult using them. Nicolas kept making us go back over areas we'd already done, telling us it wasn't clean enough. And then, when we had swept everything off the wooden floor surrounding the stage and onto the dirt floor that made up the rest of the room, he directed us in raking the loose dirt and tamping it down into a smooth, hard surface. What we couldn't tamp down, we raked out the door. Me and Mitch felt bad about doing that, but this seemed to confuse Nicolas, who wondered aloud at our reluctance to litter, and clearly had no problem dumping our garbage in the street.

"What else are we supposed to do with it?" he asked when I objected.

When I saw that we were merely adding our garbage to the festering piles already there, I didn't feel so bad, but that still didn't make it right.

After we had cleaned everything William had told us to clean, Nicolas made us clean things William hadn't told us to clean.

"We need to be useful," he said, sweeping a stairway that led to a sort of half second-story. "Our lives may depend on it."

So, we swept the stairs, raked underneath the stairs, and cleaned the corners of the room where muck had been accumulating for—from the look of it—years. We were starting to get a little fed up with him, but before he could become too obnoxious William called us back to the stage. While we had been slaving, they had been reading lines from a play William was working on. The flowery language made it confusing and hard to follow and I would have ignored it if their voices hadn't filled the room. As near as I could figure, it involved a guy called Harry and some old man with the unlikely name of Falstaff, but that wasn't the play they were putting on.

"We need to rehearse for this evening," William told us when we had gathered on the stage. "A quick meal, then back to work. You will help prepare the stage."

Godwin and Franklin disappeared, leaving William, Mendel and the three of us. We sat on the edge of the stage and ate the small portion of bread and cheese William handed out. I suspected it had been the lunch he and Mendel were supposed to share, now being split five ways instead of two. I felt a little bad about that, but I was starving, so I ate it. And William didn't seem to mind. He remained cheerful and talkative during our short rest, composing a list of jobs he wanted us to tackle in the afternoon, while Mendel kept silent. I desperately wanted to talk to him, but not in front of William, or Nicolas, and for the time being, that didn't seem possible.

After wolfing down our meagre meal, we set about ticking off the list of tasks. They were mostly simple repairs—a loose door hinge, a broken latch on the booth where the money was collected—things we fixed with a wooden mallet William had supplied. I got the impression that the maintenance of the building came secondary to their performing and preparing to perform. This gave Nicolas hope that maybe they'd let us stay for a while.

When Godwin and Franklin returned, we began setting up the stage. There wasn't much to it; there wasn't even a back wall, just a large sheet with drawings on it. We helped them hang that up, then moved all the boxes, props, and costumes behind it so they'd be out of sight. Apparently, that served as the backstage area, where the actors, who all seemed to be playing more than one role, changed costumes. It was also where the actors scanned the script, feeding lines to whoever was on stage, or did the sound effects, which involved things like hitting a box with the wooden hammer, smashing two sheets of metal together or, alarmingly, setting off a gunpowder charge. This last one wasn't practiced during the afternoon because they only had enough gunpowder to do it once, so instead they hit the metal with the hammer and pretended that was an explosion.

As we continued through our list of minor maintenance repairs, the actors ran through their lines, reading from papers as they wondered on and off the stage. The play was long and confusing, especially as Godwin or William or even Mendel would occasionally step off the stage, then back on as a different person. Throughout the rehearsals, they continued to read their lines, and wander around the empty stage, making reference to things that weren't there. It seemed doomed to fail. We listened to it, from start to finish, about three times as we continued making repairs and cleaning, but in my opinion, it never got any better, or even made any sense. Nicolas, naturally, instead of being confused by it, was thrilled.

We were still making repairs, and the actors were still rehearsing, when people began to arrive. They weren't the audience, but vendors pushing barrows filled with drinks and food. Then another man with a broad chest and thick black beard arrived. He wore a leather jacket, blue leggings and boots that ended just below his knees. He set a strong box on the counter we had stabilized, the one in the booth near the main doors, and then looked our way.

"What are these pillicocks doing here?" he bellowed.

"Ah," William said, "I see Ramsey has arrived."

Nicolas, me, and Mitch clustered around William. Nicolas tugged at his sleeve. "Who's Ramsey."

William waved his hand in Ramsey's direction. "He owns the theatre. He selects the plays. He collects the gate money and pays our wages. But …" William smiled. "He does not—"

"I do not run a charity," Ramsey shouted. "Put those urchins back on the street where they belong."

"They are not expecting money," William said. "And they are proving useful."

Ramsey started coming toward us. "They'll want to eat. And I can't imagine them being useful enough to warrant a bowl of cold pottage."

William turned to Nicolas. "I think it might be best if you went up those stairs in the back. There's a room at the top. You'll be able to see everything from there."

Nicolas grabbed us by the shoulders and pushed us toward the stairs. "Watch and learn," William called after us. Then he turned to face Ramsey's wrath.

We found the stairs and took them two at a time. There was a platform at the top, leading to a room. We ran inside and shut and bolted the door.

The room was large and dim, lit only by an opening overlooking the floor below. Cautiously, we peered out. More people were arriving, and Ramsey had retreated back to where he had left his strongbox, still shouting and waving his arms.

"What is this place?" Mitch asked.

"I think it's a public house," Nicolas said. "Or it used to be."

I looked around the room. "This must have been

the office. There's a writing desk and a stack of papers over there, and it's a good place to gander the mung."

"Will you stop talking like that," Mitch said.

"I'm just trying to fit in."

"I think it's great," Nicolas said, thumping me in the side.

"You would," Mitch said, turning to look out the window.

For some reason, I felt myself blushing.

Mitch's annoyance at my language aside, it was a good place to gander the mung, or watch the crowd, if you insist. We were all fascinated.

The rest of the high windows were fully opened, and the expansive room went from dark to merely dim. Being summer, it stayed light really late, but William and the others still had to light a few lanterns and torches to keep the room bright enough to see well. The raised platform in the centre of the room was the brightest area, and there the performers sat—William, Mendel, and the rest—waiting. It wasn't long before the room was filled with so many people, I wondered how they were all going to sit, and where.

"They stand," Nicolas told me when I asked. "Why would they sit?"

I blushed again, angry with myself for not figuring it out on my own.

The play, now that I could give it my full attention, was even more confusing. It was like nothing I had ever seen before. The actors, in various costumes, simply strutted about the stage, talking and gesturing, pretending they were in castles, or fighting battles, or lost in forests. Also, the actors who weren't on stage continued prompting those who were. Hiding behind the sheet, they whispered line after line, and the actor on stage would repeat them. I would have thought the audience would boo them off, but then the audience was like nothing I had ever seen before, either. Not only did they go along with the pretending by laughing, booing, and shouting at all the appropriate moments, but they also insulted the actors, and one another, and even got into fights, which no one bothered to break up or, in fact, seem to notice. It was chaos, with a play going on in the middle of it. The result was totally bizarre, but also, I had to admit, thrilling.

"It's marvellous," Nicolas said, leaning close to me. "This is what I came to London for."

"The words," Mitch said. "They're strange and jumbled but, if you listen hard, they do make sense."

"And even with all the noise," I said, amazed despite myself, "I can hear the actors clearly."

Nicolas stared down at the stage, his eyes shining. "It's amazing," he said, and I knew then that he would somehow find his way onto that stage, and that, wanting to impress him, I would be there with him.

Then I saw something at the edge of the crowd. I had to look twice to make sure I was seeing what I thought I was seeing. When I was sure, I turned to Nicolas to warn him, but by the size of his eyes I knew he had seen it too.

Then Mitch jumped behind us. "Duck!" he said, grabbing us by the shoulders and pulling us to the floor.

SCENE II

A Playhouse in London

MITCH

I was disappointed with the way things were going. I wanted to talk to Mendel but, in looking at the scene below, I could tell that wasn't going to happen for some time. Even as the audience continued to push into the already crowded room, the actors were busy in their makeshift backstage area checking costumes, readying the sound effects, and shuffling papers.

The crowd was so rowdy it was hard to tell when the play started, and even after it did the crowd continued to laugh and shout and argue, but the actors kept on and eventually those nearer the stage began to pay attention. Then, others in the back made their way forward so they could hear better.

At first, it was hard to make out the words, but then I understood and realized why the people near the stage were so captivated. The story was fascinating. It was about a king with a talking horse, but no one believed him except his daughter. And because William couldn't get a live horse into the playhouse, the horse was invisible, but the audience didn't seem to mind. They listened intently, hungry for the next word, and the next.

It made me realize what a special power I did have,

being able to read and write. It was rare here, and to have stories, to keep stories, to perform stories, someone needed to write them down.

Then I saw something at the back of the crowd that made my stomach drop. It was Lovell, and with him were two burly men, their faces obscured by felt hats pulled low. Arthur, Alfred, and a few of the other boys were with them. They began to circulate among the crowd, looking for marks, while the burley men moved slowly toward Ramsey and his strongbox. Lovell scanned the audience, the vendors, the actors, and then began to look upward.

I jumped behind Charlie and Nicolas, grabbing them by the shoulders. "Duck!"

We dropped to the floor. Nicolas looked at me, his eyes wide. "They know we're here. We have to run."

"No," Charlie said. "They suspect we're here."

"He's right," I said. "The gang is here to pick pockets. Lovell only knows what Arthur told him, so he's here to see for himself. If we stay low, he won't find us, and they'll go away."

"But you saw the men he has with him," Charlie said. "Lovell's desperate for money. He's here to steal the gate. And the gang will go away with everyone's purses."

Nicolas nodded. "We can't allow that."

I shook my head and kept hold of them. "We can't stop them. They'll kidnap us. And we can't get help from the actors, they're all busy. And even if they weren't, Lovell will spot us if we leave the room."

"But if there was a distraction," Nicolas said.

"How are we going to create a distraction?" I asked.

"We don't have to," Nicolas said. "The play will. The explosion is going to happen soon, I remember from when they were rehearsing. They will be setting off the charge. We haven't much time. Hurry."

He slipped out of my grasp, ran to the door, and crouched by the opening. Charlie and I followed.

"When the explosion happens," Nicolas said, "everyone will look toward the stage. There will be smoke. It's part of a joke, so the audience should laugh. The sound will cover us."

"Cover us doing what?" Charlie asked.

But before Nicolas could answer, a boom and a flash of light filled the hall. The audience gasped, there were a few screams, then a roar of laughter.

"Now," Nicolas said, and jumped from the landing. Charlie looked at me, then down at Nicolas, and followed, leaving me no choice but to leap off the platform into the darkness.

I landed with a thud, drowned out by the continuing laughter of the crowd. There were only a few people behind the stage and most of them were staring at the actors. Nearby, two sets of people were grappling on the floorboards. One was a couple of men fighting over a coin. The other two were kissing and, well, not fighting. Neither pair seemed bothered by the explosion or us thumping down not three feet from them. We all jumped to our feet and ran toward the stage, careful to keep the curtain between us and Lovell.

We found Mendel behind the stage, in costume, reading to one of the actors.

"Lovell's here," Charlie said as we ran up to him. "The head of the gang we were in. They're all here, bobbing purses."

"And Lovell has some men with him," Nicolas said. "He's after the gate."

Mendel peered around the curtain. "Which is Lovell?"

"The porknell, there," Charlie said, pointing. "And those two killbucks are with him."

"I'm going on in a moment," Mendel said. He looked at Nicolas. "You will have to take my place." He pulled his robe and hat off and threw them to Nicolas. "Put these on." He handed a stack of papers to Charlie. "Here, you read for him." Then he grabbed my arm and dragged me to the other end of the stage, where Franklin was feeding lines to William. He took the pages from Franklin's hands and gave them to me. "You read for William. He's playing the part of the King. Franklin, with me." Then he grabbed Godwin. "You come too."

They ran around the backdrop and into the audience, squeezing and pushing their way toward Ramsey.

The stage went quiet. William stopped pacing. He stood near where I was, waiting. For what, I didn't know. Every second seemed an eternity. I looked at Charlie and shrugged. He shook his head and I felt sweat begin to roll down my back. The crowd started to chuckle, then came a few boos. Nicolas rushed over to me, pulling the ridiculously long robe up so he wouldn't trip over it. He pointed to the pages. "Read."

"But what if it's not the right line."

The crowd grew more restless.

"It doesn't matter. Just read."

I read the line. William turned his head toward me. "Louder," he hissed. The crowd laughed. I read the line louder, and then he took over. "That's my cue," Nicolas said. He ran back to Charlie, then climbed onto the stage, tripping over his robe.

Charlie read a line to him, and Nicolas recited it as he untangled himself from his robe and climbed to his feet. The audience laughed at him, but at least they stopped booing.

William carried on, as if nothing out of the ordinary was happening, while Charlie fed Nicolas his lines. Nicolas, after a few stammers and stutters, began hamming it up, swishing his comically large robe around and gesturing with exaggerated movements, much to the amusement of the crowd. They began laughing so loud Charlie had a hard time shouting his lines to him.

I peeked around the curtain and saw there was a scuffle going on behind the audience. Ramsey, Mendel and the other actors, assisted by some men from the audience, had Lovell and his cronies pinned to the wall. The boys were struggling with other members of the audience and, one by one, being ejected from the playhouse.

Suddenly, I noticed the silence on stage. I scrambled to find the line.

"Look here, it's Helewis, returned from her journey," I whispered.

William turned toward the rear of the stage. "Look here," he said, sweeping his arm. "It's Helewis, returned from her journey."

The silence was so deep I could hear Ramsey's voice as he berated Lovell. William swept his arm again. "It's Helewis."

The audience began to chuckle. I looked at Charlie. "Who's playing Helewis?"

"I don't know," he said. "There's no one back here, is there?"

"Then you do it."

"How? Who's going to feed me lines?"

"Take the pages with you."

"But Helewis is a girl!"

"So, talk in a high voice, just go."

The audience roared as William swept his arm a third time. "It's Helewis, returned—"

SCENE III

A Playhouse in London

CHARLIE

"I am here, my Lord," I shouted, still standing backstage. William stopped and looked in my direction, a hint of panic in his eyes. Mitch waved his arms, urging me to go on, and even Nicholas turned my way, mouthing, "Come on."

But I couldn't move. My hands were shaking, my mouth was dry, and I found it hard to draw a breath. Then Nicolas was there, his hand stretched out to me. "Helewis, how good of you to come. Here, let me assist you into the chamber."

With that, he pulled me up onto the stage. I staggered forward, tripped on his robe and we both fell flat, the papers I had been holding scattered around us.

The audience howled and cheered. We grabbed up the papers and I tried to put them in order. William stared at us, but he was no longer panicked. He seemed amused.

It felt an age before I found my place. The audience was still laughing, so I shouted my line to be heard over them. And then the play went on.

Nicolas made the most of it, swishing his robes and gesturing, so I followed his lead talking in a ridiculously high voice and pretending to flip my long hair away from my face. William saw what we were doing and began to work with us, helping us draw as much humour from the situation as we could.

We mostly followed the play, but occasionally William would feed us a line that we had to improvise responses to. Nicolas was good at that, and as I relaxed, I found I could do it too. It was just a matter of steering the conversation along a logical—or if you wanted to get a laugh—illogical path.

From time to time, I looked at the ongoing scuffle behind the crowd. The boys had all been ejected and Ramsey, along with Mendel and the others, were pushing Lovell into the street. As he passed through the door. Lovell turned and looked directly at me. I froze, and William had to repeat his line before I picked up the cue.

We continued with the play, then the audience began to laugh again, even though no one had done anything funny. I looked around and saw Franklin, dressed as a woman, striding onto the stage. He stood in front of me, reciting my next line and making shooing gestures with his hands. The audience seemed to find this funny, so instead of leaving, I started following him around the stage, reciting our lines in unison. They weren't particularly funny lines, but every time we did it, the audience practically wet themselves.

It didn't take long for Franklin to get tired of it and, just as we were starting a new line, he turned around and went for me. I ducked and ran, and he chased me around the stage a few times before I jumped backstage where Nicolas, Mitch and Mendel were waiting. I couldn't say anything to them for a few moments, not because I was out of breath, but because the applause and cheering drowned out my voice.

Then a voice did cut through the noise. "What are they doing here? I ordered these urchins to be thrown to the street.

We all turned and saw Ramsey, his fists on his hip and his face red with fury.

SCENE IV

A Playhouse in London

MITCH

Ramsey grabbed for us, but Mendel stepped in front of him.

"Out of my way, Mendel," Ramsey roared, "or you'll be out begging with them."

"You would reject your saviours," Mendel said. He spoke quietly, yet it made Ramsey stop.

"Saviours my arse!" he said. They ruined the play, and they brought their gang of thieves to pick my audience's pockets. If it gets out that people can expect to be robbed here, we will all find ourselves with begging bowls."

Then William appeared at Mendel's side. This confused me, because, according to my notes, he was still supposed to be on stage. I looked and saw Godwin playing the King, a bundle of papers in his hand.

"Ruined your play," William said, waving his hand dismissively at Ramsey. "Why, they made it marvellous."

"The audience thought it was a joke."

"It's supposed to be funny. It's a comedy."

Ramsey glared at him. "They made it a farce."

"The audience laughed. The only problem these boys caused is that tomorrow, the audience is going to expect it to be just as funny."

"I don't care. They're thieves and they'll count themselves lucky that I didn't set the guards on them."

"It was they who alerted us to the danger," Mendel said. "Without them, your audience would have gone home poorer, and you would have found yourself with your throat slit and your money gone."

Ramsey folded his arms across his chest and narrowed his eyes. Behind us, the play went on, the audience chuckled, Nicolas and Charlie shuffled their feet and Ramsey continued to stare past William and Mendel at us. Then, finally, he spoke. "See they don't eat much." And he turned and walked away.

I let my breath out, not realizing I had been holding it. William put a hand on Nicolas and Charlie's shoulders. Nicolas looked at each of us in turn, his eyes wide and shining. "Are we … are we free?"

William clapped his hands together. "Isn't it splendid? You're part of our little troupe now."

"Yes," Mendel said, looking at me and Charlie. "Together again."

"And we're safe from Lovell," Nicolas said, giving Charlie an unexpected hug. "Thank God … thank God."

Charlie gave him a tentative pat on the back. "Don't worry. Everything's all right."

"Yeah, Nicolas," I said, feeling a little embarrassed for him. Then I added, because I knew it would make him feel better, even if it meant a problem for us, "Lovell can't reach us here."

◆

Ramsey might have allowed us to stay, but he wasn't going to be easy on us. As soon as the play was over, before the audience even left, he had us cleaning out the room, sweeping and gathering up trash. The dirt floor, being hard-packed, barely absorbed the spilled beer, wine and urine. And there was also vomit, blood and stuff you usually don't see outside of a toilet. It was disgusting. We raked everything up as best we could, sloshed water over the worst of it and tamped the dirt back down so it wouldn't turn to muck.

The only good thing, which wasn't really a good thing, was that, like earlier, we just threw all the trash outside. I really didn't like doing that but, to be honest, after raking the mountain of garbage out the door, the street hardly looked any different. Then we had to scrub the stage and the wooden floor, and pack away the costumes and the props.

Mendel and William shuttered the windows and closed the skylight and, by the time we finished, we were tired and sore, and it was pitch dark. Franklin and Godwin, as well as Ramsey, had long since disappeared, so it was also quiet. William took down the final lantern and we sat with it on the edge of the stage, in a pool of flickering, yellow light, surveying the darkened room.

"A magnificent job," William said. "Simply magnificent. Ramsey will be pleased with you."

"I'm not sure Mr. Ramsey likes us very much," Charlie said.

William waved his hand as if shooing a fly. "Don't you worry about him. He's just a big growling bear. He knows what you did for him. He'll just never admit it."

"What did he do to Lovell," I asked, "and the guys, I mean, his gang of thieves."

William chuckled. "There are many more thieves in this city than there are whipping posts to tie them to, so to call the guards would have been a waste of time, as well as bad publicity. And your Lovell is a man easily cowed. Ramsey simply threw them all out, with the promise that he would see him hanged the next time he saw him or any of his gang. He will not dare return, or send his filchers, to our little theatre again."

Despite everything, I was glad to know that Arthur and the rest of the guys weren't sitting in a jail cell. Lovell, I wouldn't mind, but the guys didn't deserve it. But now there was the question of how we were going to get our cloak back, especially since I didn't want to mention it to William. He was happy enough to take us in, but if we started telling tales of magic cloaks, he might think us loony and change his mind.

Then Nicolas looked at William. "So, what happens now?"

But it was Mendel who answered, stepping from the shadows onto the stage. "Now we wait."

Nicolas turned to him. "Wait? For what?"

"But, you know, our stuff," I said, ignoring Nicolas. "Lovell is the only one who knows who has it. How are we going to find it?"

Mendel stroked his beard. "We could visit and ask him, but I don't think we'd be kindly received."

Charlie jumped to his feet. "The man he gave it to, Fordyn. He's returning to Lovell for the rest of his money. We could wait for him and take our—"

I grabbed him by the arm and shook my head.

"Our, you know, our stuff back."

Mendel pretended to peer into the darkness. "Do you have a dozen armed men hiding where I can't see them?" He looked back at Charlie and smiled. "Any excursion to your old place of residence would surely end with us as captives, or worse."

"So, what are we going to do?"

"Wait," Mendel said.

I felt like I was being slammed against an invisible wall. Charlie walked in a tight circle, beating his fists on his thighs. Nicolas went to him and placed a hand on his back.

Then William asked, "Wait for what?"

We all looked at him, but we didn't know what to tell him.

"There is a cloak," Mendel said. "A cloak, both old and new, and an amulet of power, called the Talisman, reaching back to the dawn of time, a stone made of starfire, created by the goddess Brighid, that draws its strength from The Land, and in return, protects it. These lads, bearers of the cloak, are the Guardians of the Talisman. The Talisman has been lost for many years, the cloak, mere weeks, but finding these items is of more importance than you can imagine."

I held my breath, expecting William to laugh, or declare us all insane and demand that we leave, but instead, he ran a hand through his thinning hair and looked at Mendel, his face white, his jaw slack. "This is all so strange. And it prompts me, nay, compels me, to ask, as our young friends have done, what are we going to do about it?"

Mendel looked at him, his face grim. "Wait."

"But—" Charlie began.

Mendel held up his hand. "I have told you in the past, the cloak seeks the Talisman. But the cloak seeks you, as well. So, we wait. There are unseen forces at work. We must trust them."

William smiled, then rubbed his hands together. "A mystery. How wonderful! I love a mystery."

SCENE V

A Playhouse in London

CHARLIE

That night, we all slept in the office, where the gnarled floorboards were marginally more comfortable than the packed-dirt floor of the main room. William and Mendel, apparently, always slept there, as they quickly set out their beds while the three of us looked on. Then William found a few tattered blankets for us, and we did the best we could with them. After the nightly commotions and crowded conditions of Lovell's lair, the theatre was luxuriously spacious. Even though the office was cramped, the main room loomed large and dark and silent just beyond the thin walls.

As the others gradually settled down and I felt Nicolas's even breath on my neck, telling me he was already asleep, I heard William, still moving around in the dark, punching his limp pillow in an attempt to fluff it up.

"Where do the other actors stay?" I asked, my whisper startlingly loud in the stillness.

"Oh, they have homes and families to return to," William said. "Ones nearby, at least."

"Don't you?"

"I do, a wife and three children, but they are far away, in Stratford."

"Gosh, that must suck."

He didn't answer for a long time. I heard him pulling his blankets around himself and assumed he had gone to sleep. Then he said, "By that, I take it you mean my situation is not advantageous. My family is comfortable. The money I earn from acting is doing well enough for them."

"But what about you?"

Another pause.

"I'm doing what I want, and I have the freedom to write, and one day, when I finish a play, I can sell it and make more money. I find that very advantageous, so in your vernacular, no, it doesn't suck. Not much, anyway."

◆

The days fell into a routine after that, one that began early and ended late and left us tired and sore, but content. We were all glad for the way things were working out, but Nicolas was continually awe-struck by where we had ended up.

"It's hard work," he remarked, as we were clearing the post-play muck, "but it's honest work, and there is no hangman's rope waiting for us. Visiting my kinsman's home was surely meant to be. None of this would have been possible if I hadn't met you." He said something like this to me every day, and it always made me blush.

In addition to honest work and a place to sleep, we also got food. And it wasn't bad, either. It was tasty and filling, not the maw-wallop Lovell gave us.

True to William's word, the crowd expected the play we had ruined to continue to be the farce we had turned it into. The evening after our debut, they put on an entirely different play, but then William stayed up half the night, rewriting lines. We heard him pacing the stage, muttering lines to himself, but by the morning he'd given the play a full make-over.

Nicolas and I were disappointed that he wouldn't let us play the parts we had created. Instead, the four of them took turns doing the things we had done. I have to admit, they were more polished, but me and Nicolas agreed that our performances were superior for having been fresh and improvised.

We did get to act, though. Our favourite part of the day was after breakfast and our morning chores, when William would have us run through scenes he was working on. It was a method he had been using before we had arrived, though then he had to convince Franklin and Godwin to come in on their time off to help him out.

"This is such a marvellous development," William said, the first time we tried it. "My fellow actors behaved grudgingly when they worked on my scenes, but you genuinely put your feelings into it."

We really did make an effort to bring his words to life. Or at least Nicolas did, and I tried to keep up. But whatever we were doing, it seemed to work. Whenever we improvised something that was any good, William clapped his hands to encourage us. "That's splendid, splendid," he'd say, "are you getting this down, Mitch?"

And that was another great thing. Mitch was happy with it too. He and William sat at a table on the stage, writing quills in hand, parchment scattered all around them, scribbling new lines, or taking down the spontaneous asides me and Nicolas came up with.

Because we all looked forward to it, we were up

early each day and finished our morning chores in short order, then we would all return to the stage and begin. Mendel would join us, but what he mostly did was watch and applaud. He was always smiling, and always encouraging but, as far as we could tell, not at all anxious about getting our cloak back. Oddly, that helped me relax too. I figured, if Mendel wasn't worried, he must know something we didn't.

We were having such a good time that, even though the days were long and gruelling, we still had energy enough to practice our acrobatics during the evenings, when Mitch and William were holed up in the office discussing writing.

The scenes we did were fun, but mostly forgettable. There was only that one time, the day it all came to an end, that something truly significant happened.

SCENE VI

A Playhouse in London

MITCH

It was a pleasant time, the best we had ever enjoyed on any of our adventures. Mendel did the cooking, worked with the actors, performed every evening, and didn't appear concerned about Lovell, our cloak, or the Talisman in the least. Charlie was having too much fun playing at acting, doing acrobatics, and generally palling around with Nicolas to worry. And Nicolas, for want of a better word, seemed smitten with Charlie, practically giddy over their friendship, always with him, and always resting a proprietary hand on Charlie's arm whenever I came near. This might have annoyed me— it had always been Charlie and me, but now it was Charlie and Nicolas, and me—if I hadn't been having such a good time working with William, which sorta made it Charlie and Nicolas, and William and me.

I don't believe Charlie and Nicolas thought much about that, and the truth was, I didn't either. What we mostly thought about—because we were still having trouble believing it—was that we were free, doing what we wanted, and getting food and lodging for our labour. Our past troubles melted away and it seemed as if this was all we had known, which lulled Charlie and Nicolas into a soporific state. I knew it was too good to last, however. When Fordyn returned to exact payment from Lovell, he might kill him, and that would be the end of our tenuous link to the cloak. Something needed to be done before that happened.

But Mendel seemed content to wait so, along with the others, I waited, but I worried.

Well, not all the time. It took me a while to get over the idea that I was working with William Shakespeare as his scribe, but eventually we settled into a good routine, and I found myself arguing with him over lines and scenes. It was thrilling to watch his mind at work, and occasionally nudge him in the direction I knew it should be going. But it was also maddening to see him so unsure of himself and prone to procrastination.

"I've got a lot of disconnected scenes," he told me more than once, "but I haven't yet been able to put them all together into a coherent play." This usually happened while we sat at his writing desk in the late evenings, going over the day's notes. He would puff on his clay pipe, stare at the disjointed scenes, and sigh. "That's where the money is. If I could write and sell plays, I'd make more than if I remain just an actor. I could start my own company and perform my own work. How splendid would that be?" Then he would stare off into space. "Maybe even buy my own theatre. Could you imagine? Not having to answer to the likes of Ramsey."

"Well first you have to finish a play," I would say, not bothering to disguise the frustration in my voice.

Then William would shrug. "Oh, it's such a long shot. It will probably never happen for me."

"Not if you don't finish anything!"

"I would … I will … if I can just find the right theme."

Mendel would look on these arguments with a smile, and I would shake my head and try to get him to focus on the scenes we were working on. It was, as I said, maddening, but satisfying at the same time.

One day, while we were working in the office and Mendel was downstairs watching Charlie and Nicolas practice their acrobatics, William put his pen down and looked at me. "Your friend," he said. "He's a bit strange, is he not?"

"Nicolas?" I said, continuing to write. "No, he's fine, just a little—"

"No, I mean your friend Mendel. What is he?"

I stopped writing. "We've only met him a few times, but he's good to us. You probably know him better than we do. He's in your acting company, after all."

William shook his head. "I know very little about him. He came to me only a few days before you arrived. I took him on, not because he's a good actor, which he is, but because he can memorize lines faster than anyone I have ever met, and he's a great cook. But I always got the impression that, even though he acted in our plays, it wasn't the reason he was here."

"No," I said. "He was waiting for us. He's like that, always appearing when we need him. He helps us, he teaches us, but he always wants us to do something for him."

William raised his eyebrows. "Something, like what?"

"Something dangerous. That's why we're both glad to see him, and worried."

William stared into the distance for a moment, then shook his head and smiled. "He is a bit enigmatic, is he not?"

"Enig what?"

"Mysterious. He waited for you, and now he has us all waiting for something else. I suppose, in a strange way, that puts him in charge."

"Yes," I said. "I just wish the wait was over."

We didn't have to wait long. The next morning was our final day, although we didn't know it at the time. We were, as usual, on the stage, me and William sitting on stools at a rickety table covered in pages of parchment, Mendel sitting cross-legged on the boards and Charlie and Nicolas performing the scenes. I was particularly distracted on that day. I knew that the night before Fordyn had visited Lovell, and I couldn't stop imagining what might have happened. Then Ramsey arrived with distressing news.

We were finishing up a scene when the doors slammed open, making us all jump. Having imagined Lovell and a gang of cut-throats coming for us, I was pleased to see it was Ramsey. But only just.

He glared at the five of us clustered on the stage. "What is going on here?" he bellowed. "I am not paying you to sit on your arses all day."

William stood. "Our work is finished for now. This is rehearsal."

"Then where are the actors?"

"Godwin and Franklin are not due until noon. We are working on some new lines."

Ramsey was now at the edge of the stage, his arms folded across his chest. "Never mind the excuses, Will, it doesn't matter. The playhouse is closed."

We all, with the exception of Mendel, gaped at him.

"What?"

"Why?"

"How?"

Ramsey dropped his arms to his side, turned and

walked toward the open door. "Orders of the City Council. Plague outbreak in the Aldgate district. All places of public gatherings to be closed until further notice."

As he reached the door, William called to him. "What about us?"

"That's no concern of mine." He stepped through the door and turned to face us. "When the ban is lifted, the plays will go on. Until then, you can stay here and starve, or you can sit in the street and beg, it's all the same to me." Then he slammed the doors and left us in gloomy silence.

William sat and looked around in disbelief. "Why, that is simply ... splendid." He clapped his hands together. "Just think of the work we can get done. I might even finish a play."

"But what will we eat?" Charlie asked.

William, already scribbling on the parchment, waved a hand at him. "There's enough money to keep us fed for a while. Ramsey is just being a gloomy-guts. Unless the plague spreads into a major outbreak, the ban will be lifted in a week."

"And, if it does become a major outbreak?" Charlie asked.

William looked up and smiled. "Then none of us will have anything to worry about, because we will all have departed to that undiscovered country, that place from which no traveller returns." Then he turned back to his writing.

"What?" Charlie asked.

"He means we'll be dead," Nicolas said.

"But ... but ..."

Nicolas put a hand on Charlie's shoulder. "Don't worry. We're safer in here than out on the street. And now we have lots of time to practice."

"Young Nicolas is right," William said. "Worry will not buy you another minute. Enjoy your time while you can." He stood up, holding some pages out for Charlie. "A new scene I'm working on. It involves young lovers. Pick a part."

Charlie looked at the notes. "Ugh! We're supposed to be in love. How are we going to play this?"

"You played a woman before, you should be good at it," Nicolas said, winking at him.

"But I didn't have to pretend I was in love with a guy."

"Then I'll play the woman."

"But I'll still have to pretend I'm in love with a guy."

Nicolas grabbed him by the shoulders and shook him. "Yes, that's right. Pretend. Now, I'm a girl, not just a girl, the love of your life. Talk to me."

Charlie cleared his throat and looked at the notes. "Look there," he said, extending his arm toward Nicolas. "It's Juliet, fair as the dawn." He dropped his arm and turned to William.

"Look where? What am I doing? He's standing right in front of me. Why am I saying this?"

William sighed. "You fell in love with her earlier in the day and now you've sneaked into her garden and you're watching her through her window."

Charlie looked incredulous. "I'm stalking her?"

"If you mean approaching her with stealth, as one approaches a fair fawn in the forest, then yes, you are stalking her. You are in love, but you do not wish to scare her off, so tread softly. Only then will you capture her heart."

Charlie shook his head and leafed through his notes. "But I … it says here …," he turned to Nicolas. "The brightness of her cheeks would shame the stars." Then he burst out laughing. Nicolas looked hurt at first, then began to giggle along with him.

William clapped his hands together. "Enough now! Do you want to act or play the fools?"

"Sorry," Charlie said, wiping his eyes, "it's just—"

"Perhaps," Mendel said, "it might go easier if young Nicolas was dressed as a girl."

Nicolas stopped giggling. "Um …"

Charlie looked at him, his face going red. "Well, I … maybe …"

William jumped to his feet. "A splendid idea!"

And then I got an idea of my own. I grabbed a blank piece of parchment and began scribbling as quickly as I could.

"Nicolas," William said, prancing across the stage. "Hi thee to the wardrobe trunks. Charlie, help me stack these crates. It will make a platform from which your Juliet can lament her love for you while you watch from below. Will that inspire you to address the scene?"

Charlie helped him shove one of the wardrobe boxes into position. "I guess so, I mean, it can't hurt."

While they stacked the crates, I kept scribbling and by the time they were finished I was fairly certain I had got it right. I scanned the lines one last time, then got up to cross the stage, and stopped.

Nicolas was back, and William was helping him climb the three-tiered pyramid of crates. He wore a blue satin dress and headscarf and had washed his face and hands until they were nearly pink. Rouge highlighted his lips, but he had no need to powder his face; his cheeks were already glowing. When he reached the top, he stood upright and faced us. Charlie gaped up at him. He was beautiful.

William turned and when he saw Charlie he laughed. "Quite the transformation, eh? I see it has pushed all notions of foolishness from your head."

I crossed the stage, put my hand on Charlie's shoulder and tried to slip the pages to him but he just kept gaping at Nicolas. I had to shake him to make him realize I was there. "Here, take these," I said, slapping the pages against his chest. He took them and stared at them with unfocused eyes. "Listen to me. You're in love, but your families are enemies. I think most of these lines are right but just, well, go with your gut and play it up, like you always do."

Then I went to Nicolas, stepping up on the boxes to whisper her lines to her, I mean, him. "Follow Charlie's lead," I said as I stepped back onto the stage. "Use flowery language, and remember, you're in love."

As I returned to my seat, Nicolas curtsied to Charlie. "Are you able now to think of me as the object of your desire?"

William leaned close. "What were you speaking to them about?"

"I was just trying to give them some motivation," I said, looking at the table.

William smiled. "Well, I think they may have found it."

They picked up the scene then, without laughing, but after a few lines, William's brow furrowed. "What is this? Those are not the lines I wrote."

"I told them to improvise," I said. "I thought it might work."

William watched, his mouth set. Then his jaw slowly dropped. "It does work." He turned to me. "Are you getting this down?"

"Well, I—"

"Write, write, capture these ephemeral lines before they evaporate."

I started scribbling, and so did he.

I struggled to get the scene down as it unfolded, transcribing their words until my hand cramped and grew numb. Then, at the climax, I dropped my pen and stared. It had worked, but had it worked too well? I couldn't believe what I was seeing. Then William slapped me on the back. "What ho! Marvellous!" Then he laughed. "I wager you were not anticipating that outcome."

SCENE VII

A Playhouse in London

CHARLIE

I couldn't believe Nicolas could be so … pretty. I looked at Mitch's notes and then back at Nicolas. He was right, it wasn't hard to think of him as Juliet now. My face grew hot and nothing about the scene seemed funny any longer. In fact, I didn't even think of it as a scene, I wasn't acting, I was living the part. I looked at Mitch's notes and then up at Juliet, imagining myself in her back yard, watching her through her window, but not in a creepy way.

"But soft," I said. "what light through yonder window breaks? It is the east and Juliet is the sun! Arise, fair sun, and kill the envious moon, who is already sick and pale with grief."

Nicolas put his hands together and rested his head against them as if he were going to sleep. I looked at Mitch's notes. "See how she leans her cheek upon her hand. O, that I were a glove upon that hand, that I might touch that cheek!"

Then Nicolas sighed. "Ah me."

"She speaks," I said. "Speak again, bright angel."

Nicolas stood straight and gazed above me, as if he were looking into a night sky. "Romeo, Romeo, wherefore art thou Romeo? Deny thy father and refuse thy name. Or, if thou wilt not, be but sworn my love, and I'll no longer be a Capulet."

He sighed then. I checked my notes and saw I had a line, but Nicolas continued before I could start.

"You are not my enemy," he said, "only your name is. But what is in a name? We may call a flower anything we like, but it will always smell as sweet."

This time, I was ready. "I take thee at thy word," I said, calling up to him. "Call me but love, and I'll be new baptised."

Nicolas pretended to be shocked. "What sort of man art thou, screened in night, listening to my laments?"

"I know not how to tell thee who I am," I said. "My name is hateful to myself, because it is an enemy to thee."

"I know that sound," Nicolas said, looking down at me. "Art thou not Romeo, and a Montague?"

Our eyes met, and then a strange thing happened. I stepped forward, letting Mitch's papers slip from my fingers. My words, when they came, seemed to burst from inside me. "Neither, fair lady, if either displease you."

"How came thou hither?"

"On love's light wings, for nothing can hold love out."

"Then I thank the mask of night," Nicolas said, "or else I should blush for that which thou hast heard me speak." Then he sighed again. "Dost thou love me? I will take thy word. If thou dost love, pronounce it faithfully."

I struggled to remember the lines Mitch had given me, then realized I didn't care what they were. "Lady, I will swear my love by anything, on my eyes, by the moon—"

"Swear not by the moon, the inconstant moon, that monthly changes in her circled orb, lest that thy love prove likewise variable."

That stumped me and I began to panic. What if I was in love with her, I mean, him … or Juliet? How would I declare my love?

"Then what should I swear by?" I asked.

"Do not swear at all. Simply tell me, and I will believe thee."

I took a step forward, my heart pounding. Was this what being in love felt like? And, if so, who was I in love with? "By the feeling in my heart, I swear—"

Nicolas stretched out his hand. "Do not swear. Although I take joy in thee, I cannot wish you to swear, for that would be too rash, too sudden, too much like lightning, which brings day to night in a flash, but then is gone. Instead, let this bud of love become a beautiful flower, make it bloom fully with your words."

I took another step toward the platform. "Words? What words?"

Nicolas looked down and smiled. "Three words, three magical words any love-struck maiden longs to hear."

I wanted to say, "You first," but I thought that wouldn't fit in very well, so instead I tried, "Are we, then, to exchange vows? How can I be sure of yours? Will you, first, give that to me?"

"I gave thee mine before thou didst request it, and yet I wish I could take it back."

I felt a sudden stabbing in my chest. "Take it back? But why?"

Nicolas smiled again. "To give it back to thee, of course. My love is as boundless as the sea, and as deep.

The more I give, the more I have."

Our eyes locked, I moved closer to the base of the platform and climbed the first step.

Nicolas gazed at me as I took the second step. "Three words, my prince, and if thy love be honourable, all my fortunes at thy foot I'll lay, and follow thee throughout the world."

Nicolas suddenly knelt and took my face in his hands. "Three words, my prince. Say them and I am yours."

I stared at him, shocked. All my senses seemed to collide: the feel of his warm hands, the sight of the glow rising in his cheeks, his scent, and the rasping sound of his breath. My face grew hot, and my chest felt so tight I was afraid I might suffocate. "My … I … uh …"

He pulled me closer, until I felt his breath against my own lips. "Three words, Charlie, say them and I 'm yours."

And then the play suddenly seemed a thousand miles away and a hundred years ago, and the words welled up inside me, and I couldn't not say them. "I love you," I whispered.

And then he kissed me. It was soft and sweet, and I felt like I was melting, and then our arms wound awkwardly around each other as we embraced on the unstable platform. I heard Mitch gasp, and William applaud.

I pulled back from Nicolas, my head still spinning. "You're a girl," I said. "A real girl."

He, she, nodded. "Tell no one," she whispered.

I glanced to where Mitch was sitting. He was staring at me. His eyes huge. "Well, I said. "I really ought to tell my brother."

SCENE VIII

A Playhouse in London

MITCH

I couldn't believe what I was seeing. I just sat there, stunned, while William jumped to his feet, applauding madly.

"Bravo! Bravo! A wonderful performance." He looked at me. "Did you get all that down?"

"Um, most of it," I said.

Charlie and Nicolas climbed down from the platform and came over to where we were sitting. They stood uncomfortably close—Nicolas in his satin dress and Charlie in his grubby street clothes—both flushed and grinning.

"What a stunning performance," William said, clapping Nicolas on the shoulder. "You play a woman's role better than many a professional actor."

Then Mendel rose to his feet, also applauding, but not as enthusiastically as William. "There may be a reason for that," he said. He came to us and stood in front of Nicolas. "There is a time for discretion, but there comes a time for truth, as well. The time for truth has arrived."

Nicolas looked up at him, his grin gone, his mouth hanging open. "But—"

"Do not be afraid. You are among friends."

110

"What are you talking about?" William asked.

"It's me, sir," Nicolas said, looking at the floor. "My name isn't Nicolas. I'm not really suited to that name, if you get my meaning."

William stared at him. "What? Are you saying you are truly a girl?"

Nicolas, his head still bowed, nodded. I stood, knocking my stool over, relief flooding through me, followed by confusion, and then disappointment at having not seem it myself.

"You acted on my stage," William said. "You know that is a crime, do you not?"

Nicolas nodded.

"You, a girl, dressed as a boy, got on stage and fooled the crowd, fooled us?"

Nicolas nodded again. Charlie edged closer and took his, um, her hand. William, his face grim, his chin in his hand, suddenly smiled. "Well, isn't that marvellous?"

Nicolas raised her head. "You're not mad?"

William grabbed her away from Charlie and hugged her so tight I thought he might smother her. "Lord, no. What a jolly trick, a girl, pretending to be a boy, pretending to be a girl. That is simply fabulous. And to think it happened on my stage."

"Then, can I do it again?" Nicolas asked, her voice muffled in William's embrace.

He let her go and held her by the shoulders at arm's length. "Now you ask too much. You know we would all be arrested if you were found out."

"Arrested," Charlie sputtered. "For letting a girl act? What's that about?"

"There are lots of girl actors," I said. "Well, where we come from, anyway."

111

William looked at me with interest. "And where would that be"

"Wynantskill."

"I should like to visit this Wynantskill."

"Um, I think you might have to wait a while."

The girl I used to know as Nicolas backed away from William and stood at Charlie's side. Mendel watched, with that infuriating smile on his face that tells you he knows a lot more than he is letting on. "It is time," he said, sitting down on the stage once again. "Come, sit. There are truths to be revealed, pledges to make and plans to discuss."

Charlie sat near Mendel's feet, with his Juliet by his side. I went over and sat next to her. It was strange, seeing Nicolas in a dress, every inch a girl. I shook my head, still amazed. "I always thought there was something strange about you," I whispered.

"Thought," she whispered back, smiling, "but never guessed."

William folded his gangling body into a sitting position, his face beaming. He rubbed his hands together in anticipation, as if he was about to eat a tasty meal. "Mysteries to be revealed, how marvellous. This is turning into a splendid day."

"Yes, really splendid," I muttered. "Plague in the city, the theatre closed, our cloak beyond our reach—really, it couldn't get much better."

"So, fair Juliet," William continued, ignoring me. "If you are not Nicolas, then who are you?"

'Juliet' drew a breath and looked down at her hands fidgeting in her lap. "My name is Ellen Wyman. I come from Fishwick, in Lancashire. I'm the daughter of Richard Wyman, a yeoman farmer, who has betrothed me to a man of forty-five summers. So, I ran away, and dressed as a boy so I wouldn't be found, and for safety." She glanced at me and Charlie. "The rest, what I told you when we first met, is all true. I am a descendant of Aelric the Wanderer, of Sussex. He was the reason I found you. My desire to visit his birthplace led me to Horsham. I felt drawn there, and I knew who you were the moment I saw you."

"You were going to get married? Charlie asked. "You're only fourteen!"

Ellen frowned. "It is the custom. Do you not marry in your kingdom of Wyantskill?"

"Well, sure we do?"

"I would marry you, then, if we were betrothed."

Charlie blushed a deep red. "But we couldn't. It's against the law. You can't get married until you're eighteen."

"Against the law? Yet you allow women to act. Wynantskill is a very strange kingdom, indeed."

I ignored the exchange, thinking back to the family history Granddad had sent us, straining to remember the names, but all I could recall was the person at the top of the list. "Are you a descendant of the Baron, Robert Wandermyn?"

Ellen looked at me in wonder. "My mother has told me of him. He was one of our most important ancestors. I am sixteen generations descended from him."

"And he is related to Aelric?"

"Yes. He descends from Edric, Aelric's son. So my mother told me."

"And Aelric is related to Pendragon," I said, leaning forward to look at Charlie. "Do you see what that means?"

Both Charlie and Ellen stared at me blankly.

"We're related to Aelric," I said. "And to Pendragon."

Charlie's mouth dropped open. "Does that mean I'm related to, um, Ellen?"

Ellen hugged Charlie, squealing with delight. "You are my kinsman!" Then she drew away, frowning. "Are kinsmen allowed to marry in Wynantskill?"

"No," Charlie said, blushing. "Well, yes, sometimes. I guess it depends."

Ellen threw her arms around Charlie again and kissed him. "If kinsmen we be, then I would not enter Wynantskill for the earth, not even for the chance to act on a real stage. Here, we can marry."

Charlie sputtered. "Married? I told you, I'm too young."

Ellen ignored him and snuggled closer.

William clapped his hands together. "What a marvellous outcome. This would make a smashing play."

"Yes," Ellen said, resting her head on Charlie's shoulder. "The perfect story, with a perfect ending." Charlie, looking a little uncertain, took her hand.

"The story end is not yet," Mendel said. "The truth has arrived, now we must make a binding pledge before we move on to the next chapter, for peril awaits us."

"What?" Ellen asked, sitting suddenly upright. "Aren't we allowed some time to be happy, and content, and ... and safe?" She started to cry then, obliging Charlie to offer awkward comfort.

William glanced around in mild panic, like a dog who has just heard a sharp sound. "Peril?" he asked. "For all of us?"

"You knew who these boys were when you met them," Mendel said to Ellen. "So, you know they are here for a reason, and that reason involves danger, to them, to you, to The Land itself. But right now, the danger is mostly to you, and the five of us must make a handband, here and now, to never reveal your secret to another living soul."

"You mean I have to go back to being a boy?"

Mendel nodded. "You must. It is imperative for your safety if you are to follow these boys on their journey. And follow you must, for their success depends on you."

"But I ... can't we stay——?"

"We will have no choice." He looked around at each of us. "None of us. So, we must swear, now, for our own safety and the sake of The Land."

He held out his right hand. We all stared at it, then I rested my hand on top of his. One by one the others did the same, William last.

"From this moment on," Mendel said, "Ellen becomes Nicolas, and no one must know any different. The charge is upon her to keep her disguise, and upon us to keep her secret. To break this bond will mean death for us all."

William gulped, but said "I swear," with the rest of us. When we withdrew our hands, he took a deep breath. "This is an interesting turn of events. I must make something of this, it is all so marvellously mysterious."

Mendel nodded toward Ellen. "Go now, return to your male clothes. Dirty your face and hands. Become Nicolas again. And do so quickly."

Ellen stood and smoothed out her dress. Then she pulled Charlie to his feet and hugged him. "I fear you won't love me when I returned," she said.

Charlie kissed her. "It will take more than men's

clothes and a dirty face."

I rolled my eyes and stuck my finger in my open mouth, pretending to gag. William applauded again. "Splendid," he said. "What a marvellous scene. I'll have to work that into a play."

Ellen and Charlie looked at the floor.

"You, most of all, must guard yourselves," Mendel said to them. "Your feelings give you away. The oath we took was not a mystical vow that will bring celestial vengeance if broken. It is real. To be found out will mean death for us all. Heed this, and keep your love well hidden."

"We will," Ellen said. She gave Charlie another hug and left. Charlie watched her until she disappeared into the shadows, then he sat sullenly on the stage.

"You know something," I said to Mendel.

"I know human nature," he said. "And I know that Lovell is a coward, and a thief. Tell me, do you believe he has the money Fordyn is demanding?"

I thought about that for a moment. "I think, even if he did have it, he would hide it so he wouldn't have to give it to Fordyn."

Mendel nodded. "So do I. But if he did, how would he escape Fordyn's wrath?"

"He could slip away when Fordyn came to visit."

Mendel shook his head. "He knows Fordyn would find him."

The room grew quiet. Mendel said nothing more. Soon, Ellen returned, dressed as Nicolas, her face and hands smeared with dirt, her hair dishevelled and partially stuffed under a battered felt cap. She slumped down next to Charlie, and they gave each other the briefest of looks.

Outside I heard shouts and cheering and the

tramping of horse hooves. I looked at Mendel. "He used us," I said.

"Ah," Mendel said, smiling. "It comes to you at last."

"Lovell knew we were here, and he traded that information to Fordyn."

"And what is the logical outcome of that?"

I heard pounding on the door and a voice shouting, "Open in the name of the Queen!"

I looked at the floor, trying to quell my rising panic.

Then Mendel said, "The cloak is coming to us."

ACT III

SCENE I

An army on the march

CHARLIE

And that's how we found ourselves in the army. Again.

The men pounding on the doors didn't wait for us to invite them in. They battered them open, and in moments, the quiet room echoed with the thudding rhythm of marching feet as a short column of soldiers entered, wearing chain mail, breast plates and helmets. Each was carrying a short lance and wearing a broadsword. They marched by twos and, leading them, was Fordyn, his armour shining, our cloak draped around his shoulders. He carried no lance, but his hand rested on the hilt of his sword. He strode to the edge of the stage where the skylight illuminated him better, revealing his thin face, hard eyes, and long black hair.

"I have it there are able-bodied men idling their days away in here while others toil in defence of the realm."

William stood. "We are not idle. We are actors."

"I should put you in irons for that offense alone," Fordyn barked. "But I need warm bodies." He looked at me and Ellen and then at Mitch. "And I want these boys. On your feet, all of you."

We stood. Fordyn looked at Mendel. "The Spanish will make short work of you," he said, "if you survive the march. I expect you will be more trouble than you are worth, but I have it that you are a meddlesome old fool, so you will come with me. Now stand straight, all of you."

That was when I knew for certain it was Lovell who had sent Fordyn after us. Mendel had been leading the group that had ejected Lovell and his gang from the theatre. Lovell didn't simply want to save his skin by turning us over to Fordyn, he wanted revenge, as well.

We lined up. Fordyn shook his head in disgust. "In the Queen's name," he said, his voice booming through the empty room, "you are commanded to march with me to do battle with her enemies, and to defeat them or die. Get your weapons and follow."

"But we have no weapons," I said.

"Then you will have to pick them off dead Spaniards," he said, turning abruptly and marching between the men behind him. When he reached the end of the column, the soldiers did an about-face and marched after him. "Follow," he commanded, as they neared the door. "And stay close, I'll not have you straggling."

"How splendid," William said, jumping off the stage. "Soldiering. What an opportunity. I'll get lots of material from this."

We all joined him, following the soldiers out of the playhouse. A soldier was waiting outside, holding a horse. Fordyn mounted it without a word and trotted away. We all followed.

"But, what about the plays?" Mitch asked William. "And your family, and the stuff you're working on?"

William shrugged and glanced back at the playhouse. "If the Spanish win, all of this will be gone. If we win, I'll have lots of things to write about."

"If we live," I said.

"Tisk tisk," William said. "Now who's being a gloomy-guts?"

We marched behind the short column of soldiers, near the front where Fordyn rode, while behind us more soldiers, both mounted and on foot, snaked through the narrow lanes.

Where space permitted, people gathered to gawp and cheer. Among them I spotted Lovell and a few of the boys. They were, no doubt, taking advantage of the situation by picking as many pockets as possible, but Lovell took time out from his thieving to look our way and smile. I looked his way and held up my middle finger, but he didn't react at all.

"What are you doing that for?" Ellen asked.

"It means, well, it's an insult."

"If you want to insult him, do this." She looked at Lovell, hooked her thumbnail behind her upper front teeth and flicked it forward, making a small click.

Lovell's smile faltered, and he made the gestured back to her. Ellen laughed, then held up her middle finger. "Is this really an insult where you come from?"

"Yes, and it's a pretty bad one."

"Oh, good," she said, and showed it to Lovell one last time before we turned a corner and left him, the boys, his den of thieves, and the theatre behind.

It took a long time for the column to wind through the narrow lanes, especially as we kept stopping so they could recruit more men. Some came willingly, others had to be persuaded, and there was hardly a weapon more dangerous than a hoe among the lot of them. The conscripts were interspersed among the soldiers, most likely so they wouldn't slip away as we marched through the maze of streets. There was no chance of us doing that because Fordyn ordered a column of soldiers to march on either side of us.

It had not yet gone noon when Fordyn took us, but it was nearly three o'clock before we made it to the city walls. William, who had been busy talking to anyone who would tolerate him, told us that the place we were heading for—an army encampment about twenty miles down the river—was to the east, but the Aldgate, and the neighbourhood surrounding it, was off limits due to the plague outbreak. We were glad to avoid that, but going north instead of east meant a longer march.

When our swelling group of conscripts finally left the city, we did so by squeezing through a narrow archway in another castle-like structure built into the walls—William called it the Bishops Gate—on a cobbled road heading north. I imagined it was the same road Harold had used to march his army to York. That had been a year ago, or five hundred years ago, depending on how you look at it.

The road was wide enough, and in fair condition, considering its age. Efforts had been made to repair it over the centuries, which had only made it worse, but it was firmer and broader than the city streets and I was glad to be out in the relatively open air. I could see Ellen felt the same, she breathed the air and gazed into the distance at the first greenery we'd seen in nearly a month.

It took a while to get to the greenery, however. The area immediately outside the city walls looked pretty much like the area immediately inside the city walls: all ramshackle buildings piled atop one another, narrow lanes heaped with garbage, and everywhere people haggling, buying, selling, arguing. I turned away and, like Ellen, stared with longing into the distance.

Soon, this chaotic cluster gave way to smaller buildings, and then to what can best be described as shacks, usually with a woman in a drab dress out front chopping wood while barefoot children wrestled in the dirt. Finally, the shanties themselves grew sparse and the fields and farmland began.

Just as we were falling into an easy pace, Fordyn raised his hand and we all stopped. Then we turned east, off the broad road, to travel on rutted lanes, narrow foot paths and, occasionally, open land. The mounted soldiers negotiated this well enough, but it was tiring. Mendel, as always, walked with casual ease, as if he was strolling through a park. Me and Mitch stumbled a bit, but at least our clothes and shoes were sturdy and suited to travel. William, on the other hand, had his fancy clothes on, and thin, leather shoes, which were already showing signs of wear. Even so, he endured it all with good humour. He stumbled, but not much more than me and Mitch, and kept looking around as if he was mentally taking notes. "Marvellous," he would mutter occasionally, or "Splendid!"

Ellen—a country girl and used to rough ground—easily kept pace with the soldiers. In fact, she seemed to be enjoying herself.

We walked for about two hours, until we came to the road running east from Aldgate, where we regrouped. There was a surprising number of us: a dozen or more mounted soldiers, nearly a hundred foot soldiers, and half again as many civilian conscripts. When all were accounted for, we marched east, with the five of us directly behind Fordyn, surrounded by his guards.

"We should have joined this road earlier." Mitch

said. "We could have circled around the city easily enough. It would have saved a lot of time."

"I suspect they fear the plague," Mendel answered. "Simply being outside the walls might have kept Fordyn and his men safe, but not joining the road until it was well away from the city would be safer. You never know if any travellers might be infected."

I shuddered and looked at Ellen. "Can the plague get us out here?"

See looked at me, perplexed. "Why are you so nervous? Don't you have plague in Wynantskill?"

"Well, no. Not for hundreds of years. So, I don't know much about it. How safe are we?"

She shrugged. "You're never truly safe, but we're safe enough. This isn't what I would have wished for, but it could be a blessing in disguise. We're out of the city, in the fresh air, safe from Lovell—"

"And prisoners of Fordyn."

She smiled. "You're so pessimistic." Then she added, "I wish I could kiss you."

I looked at the road. "Me too, but please don't."

After another hour of marching, we came to a large field where a thousand or more soldiers were making camp. As we approached, several soldiers, officers by the look of their gleaming armour, assembled to greet us.

"Hail, Lord Fordyn," one of them called. "Most of our friends are here. Many more are on the way."

"I bring eight score," Fordyn said, "many loyal to our cause, and others who will fight who we tell them to."

"And others are on their way," another of the officers said. "By morning, our numbers will be half as many as Sir Dudley's army. He will be pleased at our arrival."

Fordyn nodded. "We will rest here until all are gathered." He swept his arm behind him, indicating us. "These five, put them to work, but keep them near my tent, I do not want them far from my sight."

"My lord," the men said, and came for us.

William, his clothing torn and dirty, his shoes flapping on his feet, strode forward to meet them. I looked at Ellen and Mitch, and we followed. Mendel came behind us.

"We are well met," William said, bowing to the approaching soldiers. "And willing servants all."

The soldiers grabbed him by his arms, dragging him forward. The others came for us, and we allowed ourselves to be dragged into the camp, while William protested. "Good sirs, this rough treatment does not become you. We are neither prisoners nor slaves, but brothers in arms …"

Everyone ignored him.

SCENE II

An army camp outside London

MITCH

Once our guards put us to work, Charlie and I had the advantage over Ellen. Having been conscripts in Harold's army, we knew about military life, so we made ourselves useful, and helped Ellen negotiate the chaos that is an army camp. Likewise, Mendel mentored William, and all of us worked together, erecting tents, digging trenches, gathering wood, and building cooking fires. Our competence was such that, although we were obviously prisoners, we were largely left alone, unlike some of the other citizen soldiers who were treated brutally by the regulars.

It was early evening before sporadic groups of soldiers, citizens and supply wagons stopped trickling into the field. By then the camp was a muddle of tents, flags, men, horses, and billowing smoke. Fortunately, it had not rained for a few days, so the ground didn't turn into a morass of mud. Instead, it became hard-packed and dusty, sending up clouds of brown mist, covering everything in a fine layer of grit. Ellen and William were both wide-eyed with wonder and we had a job keeping them busy enough to not draw the attention of our keepers.

As the sky grew dim and we finished our evening

meal, Fordyn greeted the leaders of the various units. One by one they arrived at his tent, identifiable by its size, ostentation, and the battle standard—bearing the image of a black dragon—fluttering in the breeze. Despite their individual encampments being a short walk away, the men arrived on horseback. If they did this to display their importance, their status must have paled a little when they confronted Fordyn.

His tent was on top of a low knoll, separate from the other tents, on the highest point in the field, and he waited outside the entrance, flanked by Cuthbert and Edmond, his fists on his hips, wearing our cloak and an unmistakably regal air. Each of the men dismounted, touched a knee to the ground and remained like that, with their head bowed, until Fordyn addressed them, saying, "Rise, bold and faithful friend."

When a dozen had gathered, Fordyn gazed about the field, his eyes resting on us for a moment, then he entered his tent, followed by Cuthbert, Edmond and his twelve followers. After a few moments, two soldiers appeared and stood at attention in front of the entrance, holding lances at their sides.

It was fully dark by then and the fires were stoked. We sat at the one nearest to Fordyn's tent, along with half a dozen of his soldiers. No one paid us much attention, but we knew if we tried to leave, we would be stopped.

We sat together at the campfire, me and Ellen and Charlie, with William and Mendel nearby, all of us watching Fordyn's tent. I didn't know what they were up to: I only knew one thing for certain. I leaned across Ellen to whisper in Charlie's ear. "Our cloak is in that tent."

"So, what are we going to do about it?" he asked. "We can't exactly invite ourselves in."

"We need some sort of distraction," I said. "Then we can slip away and go have a look."

Charlie looked around at the soldiers, the guards, and the tent, exposed on the knoll. "It would take a hell of a distraction."

Ellen pushed me away. "He'll kill you if he catches you," she said, leaning close to Charlie. "Nothing can be that important."

I shook my head. "He has our cloak. And he's obviously up to something."

"He's right," Mendel said to Ellen. "What Fordyn is brewing in his lair may be of great interest to us."

"But it's still not possible," Ellen said.

William bent toward us. "You need a distraction?" he asked. "Perhaps we can supply one." He grabbed Ellen's hand and pulled her to her feet. "Come with me, the three of you."

We walked toward the fire. The ring of soldiers watched us, mostly with boredom, some with animosity. William faced them, slowly turning as he talked, as if he were in a theatre in the round, which I suppose he was.

"My friends," he said, his voice cutting through the darkness, "why sit thee with tedium as your companion when such entertainments are at hand? These young boys can thrill you with acrobatic feats never before seen, and I can recite poetry for your edification."

The soldiers shouted and booed. I was afraid they might start throwing things, and all they had to hand were spears. William turned to us. "Perform your acrobatics. Pay no attention to them."

So, we started our act. Ellen and Charlie, anyway. I

just stayed out of the way. Soon, the crowd stopped howling at us and began to watch. Ellen did her best tricks, with Charlie helping as well as he could, which I have to admit was pretty impressive. Their routine was a lot slicker now, and entertaining enough that more soldiers and conscripts came to our fire. Soon, there were so many we had to enlarge the circle and build the fire up to throw enough light. Problem was, it threw a lot of heat, and we were sweating and exhausted before long. Then we did the finale.

"Gentleman," Ellen said, walking around the circle. She pointed to the bonfire. "As a final act, I will leap over that fire."

There was sporadic applause, and a few cheers, and Ellen came to us. "Let's do it," she said. "And make sure you do it right, or I'll be charred meat."

"Ellen," Charlie whispered, "are you sure—"

She laid her hand on his arm. "I'll be fine. But a lot of that depends on you."

She walked away then and we readied ourselves near the fire. It felt like a blast furnace. We were dripping with sweat and nearly mad with the need to get away from the flames. If our sweat-slicked hands slipped, if we didn't push hard enough, if we missed—it didn't bear thinking about. Ellen faced us and nodded. We nodded in return. The crowd watched in silence.

She loped toward us, then broke into a run, racing forward, toward us, and the flames. We readied ourselves, joined our hands, bent our knees. Then she jumped. We caught her, pushed skyward, and she sprang from our hands, heading into the inferno.

She did her flip, entering the top of the flames with her head down, then disappeared from our sight. We raced around to find her on her feet, her felt hat in her hands, comically batting at her singed hair while the crowd laughed. We ran to her and the three of us embraced. "You made it," Charlie said. "I was so worried."

She slapped him on the arm. "No faith," she said. "In me or yourself."

Then William was at our side. "Can we have some applause for these intrepid boys," he said, "as I assume you will not be throwing coins."

The crowd laughed and applauded, and we took a bow.

"Come," he said, leading us through the ring of soldiers. "You must be very thirsty. Here, Mendel, find these boys refreshment while I entertain our fine companions."

He pranced back into the circle, illuminated by the fire, and began reciting. He was met with a few boos, but soon the crowd quieted again.

"Those are rather bawdy verses," Ellen said.

"He knows his audience," I said. Behind us, the crowd laughed. Mendel led us just beyond the circle and we waited. No one was watching us. They were all listening to William as he strutted around the fire, gesturing to the crowd, his fine clothes muddied and ragged, his broken shoes flapping on his feet.

"Now is your chance," Mendel said. "You and Charlie go. Ellen, you stay with me. If someone does look our way, it will be good to have at least one of you with me."

"But Charlie—" Ellen said.

"But, our drink," I said.

Mendel shook his head and pulled Ellen after him as he returned to the fire.

"Go," he said.

SCENE III

An army camp outside London

CHARLIE

We crept away from the ring of soldiers, into the darkness where the guards in front of the tent couldn't see us. We crept in a wide circle around the knoll, and when we were behind it, we approached the tent.

"No guards," Mitch said, peering into the gloom.

I looked at the rear of the tent, and the slope of the knoll. No one was in sight. "He wouldn't expect anyone to be here," I said, hoping I wasn't being too optimistic.

We crawled up the knoll, to the back of the tent. There were voices inside, but we couldn't make them out. Carefully, slowly, we lifted the bottom edge of the tent about an inch and peered through the gap.

The interior of the tent was bright, lit by numerous torches, but directly in front of us was a wooden platform. It blocked our view of the people inside, but it also kept them from seeing us. Encouraged, we lifted the canvas higher and eased our heads under, craning our necks so we could see above the platform. Even then, all we could see was the top half of an ornate wooden chair, where Fordyn—still wearing our cloak—sat, talking to the men gathered in front of him. At least, we assumed it was the men, because the platform still blocked most of our view. All we could do was listen. So, we waited. I concentrated on the voices in the room instead of the pounding of my heart, and soon I heard one of Fordyn's followers talking.

"... the Earl of Leicester's troops still outnumber ours by almost two to one."

Fordyn shifted in his chair. "That's what I have you for. During the days we are there, you are to circulate among his soldiers, feel them out, find ones sympathetic to our cause. If it comes to a fight, his troops will be divided. But I do not expect him to attack. By the time he realizes what is happening, it will be over, and he will understand where his loyalties lie."

"But he may respond with speed," the man said. "What will we do if that happens? And, of course, there is still the Duke of Parma and his Spanish soldiers to consider."

Fordyn leaned forward. "Are you not with me? Have you no faith?"

"Yes, yes I do, Lord Fordyn," the man said. "But prudence dictates that we anticipate all scenarios."

"This is the only scenario," Fordyn said, rising to his feet and stepping forward. I raised my head as high as I dared, until I could see his head and shoulders above the back of his chair. He reached for something hanging around his neck on a silver chain and held it up. "When the Duke of Parma hears what has happened, he and his men will quake in their boots. They have the courage to attack women, but not men. And with this in my possession, we cannot fail."

"Your amulet," the man asked, "it promises victory?"

"That's the Talisman!" I whispered so loudly I was

afraid Fordyn would hear. Fortunately, he continued shouting at the man.

"It does," Fordyn said, dangling the Talisman from its chain so the black surface glowed in the torchlight. "It taps into the ancient power. You've heard the legends, now you see the reality. Whoever holds this ancient stone cannot be defeated." He allowed the Talisman to fall back against his chest. "I pledge to you, my friends, my comrades, my brothers, that your loyalty will not go unrewarded. Victory is assured. It will be swift, and it will be sweet."

Fordyn sank slowly into his seat. "All here know that. Do you?"

"I do," the man said, after a moment of hesitation.

The tent became silent then, and me and Mitch stared at each other with our mouths open, not daring to make a sound, even though we were both bursting to scream about the Talisman.

Then Fordyn spoke. "We march in the morning and will reach Tilbury before nightfall. That will give you three days to feel out the other captains and their men. I know many are sympathetic to our cause, so I expect good reports and quick progress. This is the last time, until our victory, that we will assemble like this. In the field, come to me one at a time, but strike your tents close. When our hour comes, we will join with speed— we and our confederates—and we will strike." He rose from the chair again, raising his hands like he was signalling a touchdown. "Kneel now, and swear fealty."

For a few moments, the only sound was the creaking of leather and clanking of metal. Then I heard mumbling that grew louder as—one at a time—each man swore his loyalty to Lord Fordyn. We pulled our heads out and sat in the dark.

"We've got to get back and tell Mendel," Mitch whispered.

"What do you think it means?" I asked.

"I'm not sure, but it can't be good. Let's go."

I grabbed his arm, listening to the sound of tramping feet coming from the front of the tent. "We've got to wait. The men are leaving now. They may see us."

We sat quiet, counting the seconds. Sweat began to prickle my brow. After what seemed like an eternity, I glanced at Mitch. "Do you think this is long enough?"

Mitch didn't say anything, so I began to crawl away.

"Wait," he whispered, leaning close to the tent. "They're still talking."

"Haven't we heard enough? We're going to get caught."

Mitch laid down and slowly lifted the tent wall. I sighed and crawled back to him. We both stuck our heads under. We couldn't see anyone this time. Fordyn was off his chair, but there were still a few people in the room, and Fordyn was talking to them.

"… essential to our success," he said. "They must be protected until we need them."

"As you wish, my Lord," came the voice of Cuthbert.

"But you already possess the Talisman and the cloak," Edmond said. "Surely that is enough. I find them more trouble than they are worth."

"You are short sighted and a fool," Fordyn said, his voice rising. "Tell me, how did I come by this cloak?" An uncomfortable silence followed. "Cat got your tongue? Let me remind you. It was stolen by Lovell from those boys, paid in lieu of a debt to me. And this?" We heard the rustle of the cloak and assumed he must be holding up the Talisman. "What was this bought with?"

"My Lord, please," Edmond said. "My apologies, I only meant—"

"Blood," Fordyn shouted. "Do you know how much blood was spilled for this?"

More silence. My heart nearly stopped when heavy footsteps echoed on the wooden platform. But then I heard the chair groan as Fordyn sat heavily. There was more silence, and when he spoke again his voice was quiet.

"I possess them," he said. "But not by right. This will come to haunt me. Not this year, not the next, but someday. I must legitimize myself from the start, so there can be no question of my authority. The boys must have the cloak returned to them. They are the rightful bearers of the cloak, and thereby Guardians of the Talisman. And they must present the Talisman to me in a ceremony so everyone can see it is mine by right."

"But only two of the boys are the Guardians."

"Yes, but which ones?" Fordyn asked. "That cur Lovell told me only that two of the three boys were owners of the cloak. We need to be certain who they are. There is no room for error here."

"I, well, we could ask them."

Fordyn laughed. Cuthbert and Edmond remain silent and the atmosphere in the room grew tense.

"You are too trusting," Fordyn said. "Here is how we get the truth from them. We slit the throat of the old man within their seeing. Then we hold a knife to the actor's throat and promise a similar fate unless they reveal which two of the three are the true cloak bearers."

"Yes, my Lord," Cuthbert said. "But shouldn't we kill the actor first?"

"Nay. That actor is in love with himself. With a knife to his throat, he will beseech them unashamedly. If their hearts are hard, he will soften them. And then we make the same promise to convince them to willingly present the Talisman. Until then, they are necessary. So, you will make certain they remain safe."

"And when the Talisman is presented?" Edmond asked.

"Then we kill them all."

My stomach felt like ice. I looked at Mitch. His face was white. He motioned with his eyes that we should leave.

As I pulled my head from the tent, I heard Fordyn continuing to give orders. "… and that captain, Bartholomew, who seemed doubtful of our success. See that he has an accident on the road tomorrow. He will be a liability at Tilbury. Find a replacement from within Sir Dudley's forces when we arrive …"

We said nothing. We just crawled as fast as we could down the knoll and crept around to the front. In the distance, we could see that the fire was still burning, and William was still entertaining the men.

"Gosh," I said. "He sure has a lot of material."

"I get the feeling he could go all night," Mitch said. "He loves a crowd."

As we hurried toward the fire, someone shouted to us from the shadows.

"Halt!" I heard the clatter of steel and my breath caught in my throat. A soldier in chain mail, holding a short lance, approached us. "Be ye friend or foe, stand and declare yourselves."

Mitch's voice came out in a squeak. "Friend," he

said.

"It's just us," I added

"What were you doing back there?" the soldier demanded. "Did you approach the tent of Lord Fordyn?"

I saw Mitch's face go white. He had no lie ready.

"The jakes," I said. "We needed it real bad."

The soldier stepped closer. "Not likely," he said, then gestured with his lance, pointing in the direction we had come from. "Show me where."

I shrugged. "Okay. But I warn you, we haven't been feeling very well lately, so it won't be pretty. And I'd hold your lance with one hand and your nose with the other if I were you."

The soldier hesitated. Then Mendel came up behind us and placed his hands on our shoulders. "There you are," he said. "Are you feeling better? Perhaps you'd like one of my herbal remedies. That should set you right."

The soldier lowered his lance. "Very well. Get back to your camp. And don't go wandering again."

SCENE IV

An army camp outside London

MITCH

Before we returned to the others, we told Mendel what we had learned.

"What do you think it means?" Charlie asked.

Mendel rubbed his beard. "I can't say for sure."

"Do you think he wants to take over the whole army?" I asked.

"That seems far-fetched," Charlie said.

"Don't forget," Mendel said. "He has the Talisman, and a black heart. That is a dangerous mixture. He believes he can do whatever his dark nature can conceive."

"Whatever it is," Mitch said, "we're only safe until he does it."

Mendel nodded. "Then we must be alert, cunning and prepared to act."

"We need to keep that last bit, about what Fordyn means to do to us quiet," I whispered to Charlie. "We don't want to frighten the others."

Charlie nodded but didn't get a chance to answer because Ellen rushed up and threw herself at him.

"Thanks be to God," she said, taking his face in her hands. "I was so worried, I thought I'd lost you."

Charlie grabbed her wrists and gently pulled them

down to her sides. "We're fine," he said. Then he glanced around to make sure no one was close by. "But we're in grave danger."

"Danger?" she asked. "Of what?"

"Fordyn is up to something. He and his men are staging some sort of coup after we join up with the rest of the army at some place called Tilbury."

"Treason," she whispered. "Foul dealings." She stepped away from Charlie, her hand over her mouth. "And we will be in the midst of it."

We returned to the fire. It was dying down now and William—tired but satisfied—took his final bow. When the men and soldiers began wandering back to their own camps, we crawled into the tent we had been assigned and went to sleep.

In the morning, I kicked Charlie and Ellen awake. It only took one kick, because they were practically on top of one another. After that, I went outside and stirred up the fire. Mendel was already up and had gone out foraging for breakfast. He returned about half an hour later with a sack full of roots, berries, seeds and mushrooms, and took them to the other camps to beg for a cooking pot in return for food.

Soon, we had a hot breakfast, and plenty left over, even though William ate ravenously.

"Have any reviews come in yet?" he asked between mouthfuls. "I think my performance last night was splendid. I had the crowd in the palm of my hand. It was so exhilarating." He looked at Charlie and me. "Did you see? What did you think?"

"Um, well, we were busy," Charlie said.

William shovelled more food into his mouth. "Oh yes. That business with Fordyn and his coup, and his plans for us. Treachery, double-dealing, and murder.

What a marvellous idea for a play!"

"But …," I said. "How did you—?"

"Oh, Ellen … I mean, young Nicolas here, told me. Good job getting that intelligence."

I glared at Charlie. "You told her?"

Charlie looked at the ground. "Well, what was I supposed to do. She asked."

"And you told William," I said to Ellen.

"Of course," she said. "He's one of us. He needs to know how much danger we're in."

I sighed. "Well, just don't tell anyone else."

Ellen looked at Charlie. "By the Lord above, your brother thinks me crazy." She gave his hand a surreptitious squeeze and they both giggled.

I looked around for Mendel for support, but he was gone, so I busied myself packing up our meagre supplies: a few tattered blankets, a cooking pot, two wooden bowls and three spoons.

We marched out of the field before the sun was high, after having struck all the tents and doused the fires. As usual, we were at the front of the column, near Fordyn, where he could keep an eye on us. It was awkward being under such scrutiny. I made a point of walking between Ellen and Charlie, to keep them from pawing at each other, and then concentrated on keeping up the pace. William, even with his tattered shoes and muddied clothes, had no trouble. It was easier going on the road and his mood was buoyant. Mendel walked behind us, silent, his eyes fixed on the road ahead, as if answers awaited us there.

Compared to the march to York, marching to Tilbury was a Sunday stroll. And just as boring. The only thing that happened along the way was around noon, when word came through the ranks that one of the leaders, a Captain Bartholomew, had been thrown from his horse and killed. I looked at Charlie. He said nothing, and we continued marching. In late afternoon, we came to a broad field on the edge of the Thames. The river was wide here, but it still stank of sewage.

Another army was already there. Tents, smoking fires, banners, horses, and men all gathered around a stone fort in the distance. We stopped on the outskirts and a man came riding out to greet us. He was dressed in fancy garments with light armour. Four men rode at his side.

"That's Sir Robert Dudley," William said. "The Earl of Leicester."

"Greetings, Lord Fordyn," the man said. "Have you come to help us see the Spanish off?"

Fordyn sat straight on his horse, his armour gleaming in the sun. "I have, Sir Dudley. Two thousand men are under my command, and now they are under yours."

"And the Queen's," Dudley said.

Fordyn inclined his head in acknowledgment but said nothing.

"You can set up camp here, upriver from us," Dudley said. "You can be our rear guard. We have lookouts downriver, spying for Spanish ships. When they come, we will fight them off as they try to land. If any get past us, you and your men can harry them."

"As you wish," Fordyn said, bowing to the Earl, a thin smile on his lips.

We spent the rest of the daylight setting up camp. As dusk settled, we were, once again, outside Fordyn's big tent, sitting around a fire, eating what Mendel could forage and being watched by the guards.

"I don't get it," Charlie said. "We marched all the

way out here and now we're just backup, and Fordyn doesn't seem to mind. You'd have thought he'd want to be at the front, taking all the glory."

"Maybe he's hoping the Spanish will overwhelm Dudley's army," I said. "Then he can swoop in and save the day."

Charli shook his head. "I don't think Fordyn wants Dudley humiliated, I think he wants him gone, and himself in his place."

"Do you think his intention is to take over the entire army?" Ellen asked.

"Whatever his intentions," Mendel said, "I don't believe fighting the Spanish are among them."

"And whatever his intentions," I said, "we need to get our cloak back. And retrieve the Talisman."

"I could distract the men again," William said. "Then you might get back into Fordyn's tent."

"Yeah," Charlie said. "We found a way in easily enough last night. We could sneak in that way, while he's asleep."

Ellen punched him on the arm. "You will do no such thing."

"Ow. Why not?"

"There will be guards inside, and don't think he'll leave the cloak, or the Talisman, out where you can pick them up at your convenience."

"But we could—"

"And even if you did manage to sneak them out of the tent without getting killed, we're surrounded by two thousand soldiers loyal to Fordyn. How long do you think we could hold on to them?"

Charlie crossed his arms and huffed. "I just want us to be safe again. Is that so bad?"

Ellen leaned against him. "No. I want to be safe, as

well. But we need to think of another way."

"If we find out what he's up to," I said, "that might help us."

"Perhaps some answers will come in the morning," Mendel said. "We should sleep now. It could be a busy day tomorrow."

SCENE V

An army camp at Tilbury

CHARLIE

The next morning, all we got was more work. We dug pits, made fires, tended horses, and polished armour but were no wiser about what Fordyn was up to or, more importantly, how to get our cloak back.

The Talisman was another problem. Obviously, Fordyn was not supposed to have it, and we needed to find a way to take it from him. But we had no idea what to do with it once we got it. I was sure that Mendel knew, but he didn't tell us. Not yet anyway. He tends to tell us what we need to know just before we need to know it. He's strange that way. Mitch calls him enigmatic.

And so, we worked and watched and waited.

It astounded me how easily Ellen kept up with us, as I would have thought the digging and hauling and polishing of armour would be too hard for a girl. William had a harder time of it. For all his boasting about his country upbringing, he was softer than Ellen, but he still did what was asked and somehow kept his spirits up, even as his fine clothes disintegrated around him. Mendel set himself up as cook and spent his time foraging, preparing, and cooking meals for us and the rest of the soldiers in our company.

It was a hard life, but boring, which wasn't so bad. I got to work alongside Ellen most of the time, and that was nice. It might have almost been enjoyable if it wasn't for the fact that we were prisoners and due to be executed. There wasn't a lot we could do about that, so we tried to forget it. All we could do was keep an eye out for an opportunity, but an opportunity to do what, no one—not even Mendel—could say.

Then, on our third day in the camp, as we were preparing for the noon meal, I thought I heard trumpets. Me and Ellen were kneeling in the mud at the edge of the river, scooping buckets of water from the Thames, under the watchful eyes of our guards. We were upriver from the camps because, as dirty as the water running out of London was, it was even murkier after it ran past six thousand soldiers. As the strange noise echoed down the river, I stood up and looked around. "Did you hear that?"

Ellen shook her head. Then the trumpets sounded again. Gazing upriver, she dropped her bucket and stood next to me. "That was a fanfare. And that's the royal barge. It must be the Queen."

"Get on with it," one of our guards shouted. "Fill yer buckets and get back to camp."

"The Queen's coming!" Ellen said.

"Yer daft," the guard said, while his companion laughed.

The trumpets sounded again, loud enough for some of the soldiers in the camp to hear. The guards went quiet. Their eyes widened and their jaws dropped as they stared upriver. I turned to see what they were looking at.

A broad, flat-bottomed boat, decked out in banners and flags, with men wearing fancy uniforms standing on deck, and about a dozen people rowing like galley slaves, was coming toward us on the receding tide. As the boat drew near, I saw there was a small awning in the centre of it. Under the awning was an ornate seat, and on the seat sat a woman like no woman I had ever seen before.

Although the men surrounding her were impressive in their red and gold tunics, they paled next to the woman, who literally glowed. Her face was as white as the lace ruff behind her head, and her armoured breast plate, polished to a high sheen, gave the illusion that the sun radiated from within her.

Beside me, Ellen whispered, "The Queen!"

I turned to her, but she was gone. Then I looked down and saw that she was kneeling. She reached up, grabbed me by my arm and yanked me down. "Kneel," she hissed. So, I knelt.

As the boat drew level with us, our guards grunted and sank to their knees. The men in our camp turned and, one by one, knelt as the royal barge floated by. As they neared Sir Dudley's camp, a cheer went up, and followed them along the river until they docked at the fort.

We could barely see the figures getting off the boat, but soon Ellen was satisfied that the Queen was inside the fort, and only then did she stand up.

The Queen," Ellen squealed. "Oh, my Lord, did you see that? The Queen!"

I rubbed my neck and flexed my knees. "Yes."

"Wasn't she splendid? Wasn't she glorious?"

"She was," I said. "But keep your enthusiasm to yourself. It seems out of place."

We looked around. Our guards were already standing, glaring impatiently at us to get on with our work. The soldiers in our camp had returned to their chores, stoic and grim-faced. Many were polishing their armour or sharpening their weapons. None were as flush-faced as Ellen.

Ellen's eyes narrowed as she watched them. "They should be glowing with excitement."

"Well, they're not," I said.

In the distance, the shouts and cheers of Dudley's men continued.

She bent down to pick up her bucket. "No, they most certainly are not," she said. "There's something wrong here."

"What do you mean?"

Ellen lowered her voice and leaned close. "These men, all the soldiers under Fordyn's command, are not as loyal to the Queen as they should be."

I shrugged. "Well, maybe they didn't vote for her."

Ellen shook her head. "That is … I … you don't understand. Fordyn is gathering men loyal to his cause, and none of those men seem pleased to see the Queen."

"Yeah. But like I said—"

"And didn't you tell me Fordyn said the Spanish were brave enough to fight women, but not men?

"I still don't see how—"

She grabbed me by the shoulders and shook me. "Do you not understand? Fordyn doesn't want to take over the army. He wants to take over the kingdom."

"That's crazy."

"Of course it is, but you said that special rock of yours, that Talisman, could make him crazy, make him believe that his own desires are his true destiny."

"End your argument before I do," one of our guards shouted, drawing his sword. "Now get on with it."

We knelt in the mud again and scooped murky water from the river. Our guards turned away, leading us back to camp. As we followed, I shook my head to try to clear it. Things were getting much too complicated.

"So, what are we supposed to do about it?" I asked. "Get ourselves invited into the fort?"

Ellen scowled at me. "Scoff all you like," she said, "but this is the truth: Fordyn is after the Queen, and it is up to us to protect her."

SCENE VI

An army camp at Tilbury

MITCH

Charlie and Ellen bickered the rest of the day, which made it more of an agony than usual. The Queen and her entourage stayed in the fort, so Dudley's entourage, who had been sleeping in the fort, had to sleep in the camp. Like the rest of us.

When night fell and we sat around the fire, Ellen sat with William, and Charlie sat with me, his face glum. When we went into the tent to sleep, Ellen bedded down closer to me than to Charlie so, in a huff, he went outside to sleep by the fire. They must have made up during the night, however, because when I woke in the morning, they were both in the tent, entangled under a single blanket.

To keep the peace, we avoided speculating about Fordyn's plans and instead concentrated on our tasks. Everything went back to normal, except there was more commotion around the fort than usual, and Fordyn, his loyal commanders and most of his men were gone, though we didn't know where and none of us dared to mention it.

For my part, I thought Ellen's notion was plausible, but I found it hard to believe that Fordyn, even beguiled by the Talisman, would be foolhardy enough to try to take over the Kingdom. Naturally, I kept that to myself, and we all did our best to put it out of our minds, but near midday the Queen emerged from the fort, mounted on a white horse, and she—as well as Ellen's suspicions about Fordyn—became impossible to ignore.

Dudley's soldiers stopped what they were doing and turned her way, bowing or kneeling. Then we saw a group of Fordyn's men, but not Fordyn himself, gathering behind Dudley. They stopped too, but instead of kneeling, they began gathering in tight formations. At the head of each group, mounted on horses, was one of Fordyn's eleven remaining, trusted conspirators.

The Queen moved toward Dudley's men, leaving her armed bodyguards lined up near the fort. She wore a flowing, white gown covered by a simple breastplate. On her head was a silver helmet with a large white plume, and she, herself, seemed to glow white. Even from a distance, the effect was stunning: a radiant queen flanked by Robert Dudley, the Earl of Leicester, and Robert Devereux, the Earl of Essex, (at least according to Ellen) and followed by another man (who she didn't know), all on brown horses and dressed in drab clothing that served to heighten the queen's intensity.

In front of her were three men on foot, two leading her horse, and the other, out in front, holding a ceremonial sword.

The five of us stood together, watching the spectacle. It was hard not to be awed. Mendel maintained his usual calm, but William's eyes were practically bulging from his head and Ellen watched with her mouth open. Then she turned and grabbed

Charlie by the arm. "The Queen is coming to inspect the troops. Unguarded. This is the moment." She glanced around at me, William, and Mendel. "Get ready. All of you."

Charlie pulled his arm away. "You're not going to start that again, are you? He can't possibly think—"

Then the flaps of Fordyn's tent parted and Cuthbert and Edmond strode out. Close behind was Fordyn, wearing polished armour, a helmet, and our cloak. Around his neck, suspended from a silver chain, was the Talisman.

Cuthbert held his horse and Edmond helped him mount. He sat straight in the saddle and surveyed the scene before us.

"She comes among us with little protection," he said. "Go to my men and bid them be ready. Tell them to follow my lead. Soon, England will have a proper leader. A strong leader, not a withering woman. Now go."

Cuthbert and Edmond mounted their horses and galloped down the slope to the waiting men.

Fordyn turned his gaze on us. "Guard them," he said to the dozen or so men still in the camp. "See that they remain here."

One of the soldiers, carrying a lance and wearing a broadsword, came our way.

Ellen grabbed me by the arm and pulled me next to Charlie. She looked at Charlie and then at me, her eyes wide and bright. "This is it," she said. "This is our chance. You know what to do."

ACT IV

SCENE I

An army camp at Tilbury

CHARLIE

Ellen ran. The soldier ran toward her, so we ran toward the soldier while William looked on, perplexed.

"Stop him. Stop that boy," the soldier shouted. When he saw us running straight at him, he turned our way and stood still, pointing his lance in our direction. "Come no closer, or I will run you through."

We split up. Mitch ran to the soldier's left while I circled around, coming at him from the right. He looked from me to Mitch, not certain who was the most immediate threat, and failed to see Ellen running up behind him. She threw herself at the back of his knees, taking his feet from under him. The soldier hit the ground with a thump and a clank of metal, and lay kicking and thrashing like an over-turned turtle. Ellen rolled away from him and jumped to her feet. Scattered around the campsite, the other soldiers laughed.

Fordyn looked on with mounting anger. "Get them," he shouted.

"Come on," Ellen said.

We raced toward Fordyn. Ellen let us get ahead of her. We stopped near Fordyn's horse, turned, and saw Ellen running toward us. Mitch and I clasped hands,

Ellen leaped. We caught her and vaulted her high, toward Fordyn, who had no time to react. As Ellen flew at him, he tried to draw his sword, but she somersaulted over his head before it was halfway out of its scabbard. And as she passed over Fordyn, she grabbed the Talisman, jerking Fordyn so roughly he nearly fell from his horse. Then the chain snapped, and Ellen landed awkwardly, tumbling to the ground with the Talisman in her hand.

"Get him!" Fordyn shouted, his voice on the edge of panic.

Ellen rose to her knees as two soldiers descended upon her. She turned toward us just as they pounced. "Charlie!" she said, throwing the Talisman at me. The soldiers tackled her. I started to run to help her, but as they wrestled her to the ground, she shouted at me: "Go! Take it to the Queen!"

I grabbed the Talisman, turned, and ran. Behind us, Fordyn shouted at the men holding Ellen. "Leave him, you fools. Get the amulet!"

There may have been only a handful of soldiers in Fordyn's camp, but they were all after us. I dodged between them and ran around them but couldn't shake them off. Ahead, just outside of Fordyn's camp, all the other soldiers were facing the other way, watching the Queen and paying no attention to us. If I could get to them, I could hide, and more easily dodge Fordyn's men, but just before I reached them, a heavy hand fell on my shoulder and brought me to the ground.

"Mitch," I shouted, throwing the Talisman his way. It arced toward Mitch and, to my surprise, he caught it. I felt relief, even as the soldier pressed me to the ground. Then I saw another soldier go for Mitch.

"Leave him. Get this one," someone shouted. The

soldier let me go, running from me toward Mitch. I jumped up and ran after them.

Mitch dodged around horses and men, heading for the other camps and the Queen. The soldiers were right behind him, though, and in moments one of them grabbed him by the collar.

"Mitch," I shouted as they dragged him to the ground. "I'm here."

Without looking, he flung the Talisman over his head. The soldiers let go of him and chased after it. I watched it flip through the air and dove for it when it landed. I had it in my hand and was getting to my feet when I heard soldiers rushing up behind me. Then someone called: "Charlie, over here."

I looked toward the voice. It was William. I threw the Talisman to him and then fell to the ground as a soldier slammed into my back. The world went dark. I saw stars and felt pain in every muscle in my body. I prepared myself for more pummelling, but suddenly they were off me. I shook my head and sat up. They were now running after William. Someone else ran past me, shouting, "Come on." It was Ellen. I got to my feet and ran after her.

The soldiers were already closing in on William. He dodged left and right to put them off, but they were on him before we could catch up. The soldiers piled on top of him, two, three, four. We ran faster. Then Mitch came in from the right. He was close to the pile but there was nothing he could do. Then, from between William's legs, which were all we could see of him by now, a hand appeared, holding the Talisman. Mitch grabbed it and ran.

With the soldiers close behind him, Mitch ducked under horses and dodged around carts. Ellen and I raced after him. We were getting closer to the Queen now, so the crowd was thickening, making it harder to move, and impossible to see where Mitch was. The only landmark we could see was the Queen. So, we ran toward her.

Then the crowd thinned abruptly, and an open space appeared; a gap formed by the respectful distance the men kept from the Queen. The three of us ran into the gap with our pursuers close behind. The Queen's guards, seeing what was happening, quickly formed a protective line in front of her horse. Still, we ran toward them. They brought their lances up, pointing them at us.

"Nicolas," Mitch said. Then he tossed the Talisman to her. She nodded and let us get ahead of her. We were tired, all of us. My body ached from the repeated tackles, Ellen was limping, and Mitch was gasping for breath. Ahead of us, a line of the Queen's soldiers stood in a solid wall bristling with lances. Behind us, Fordyn's soldiers closed in. There was going to be no room for error, or a second chance.

Then Fordyn rode into the gap, sending soldiers scattering before his galloping horse. "Lances up!" he shouted to the Queen's Guards. "They are going to vault the assassin over your heads!"

The lances went up. We would have to throw Ellen higher than we ever had. We stopped short of the Guards, where they couldn't reach us. I grabbed Mitch's hands. He looked at me, panicked.

"We can't do this," he said. "She won't make it."

SCENE II

An army camp at Tilbury

MITCH

Ellen ran toward us, never slowing, never hesitating. I looked toward the Queen's guards and the barrier of lances, sharp and deadly, higher than the bonfire we had barely been able to vault her over. I braced myself and looked at Charlie. The panic in his eyes told me he knew as well as I did that we were throwing her to her death. Then, as Ellen came near, she shouted, "Break!"

We dropped our hands and ran as Ellen dove between the legs of the guards. They tried to catch her, but she squirmed away. They turned, scrambling for her, and I raced around the line just as the first one tackled her to the ground. I jumped on his back, and another guard jumped on mine. I saw Charlie rushing in. He dove on the pile and another guard landed on top of him. I struggled, trying to free myself but hands grabbed my arms and legs.

The guards shouted and cursed and, from further away I heard the crowd roaring and Fordyn shouting. Then a slender arm slithered out from beneath the tangled pile of bodies as Ellen raised the Talisman as high as she could.

"Your Majesty," she shouted. "I have the Talisman."

SCENE III

With the Queen's Entourage

CHARLIE

My face was half pushed into the dirt, but I strained my neck to see Ellen, holding the Talisman, and the soldiers raising their swords. I would have screamed at them, but my mouth was full of mud.

Then the Queen looked down. Sitting high on her horse, with her pale face and shining armour, she seemed to be the only one who wasn't panicking.

"Hold!" she said. "Bring them to me."

The soldiers lowered their swords, but kept a tight grip on us, hauling us to our feet. Another soldier dragged William forward and the four of us were pushed—muddy, bloody and with spears poking at our backs—to stand in front of the Queen.

"Traitors," the crowd shouted. "Kill them."

The Queen raised her hand, and the crowd went silent.

"I have heard legends of the Talisman," she said, looking at Ellen. "But in those tales, the Guardians of the Talisman are brave knights, and never such a slight boy as yourself."

Ellen blushed, started to curtsy, then bowed. "Your Majesty, I beg your pardon. I am not the Guardian." She waved her hand toward me and Mitch. "They are."

The Queen's red lips rose in a humourless smile. "Ah, so you are the knights, the Guardians, the cloak bearers. Pray, where is your cloak?"

Before Mitch could say something polite, I pointed at Fordyn. "He's wearing it," I said. "A thief named Lovell stole it from us, and Fordyn took it from Lovell in payment for a debt. But it belongs to us."

Fordyn glared at us. Then bowed his head to the Queen. "That, if you'll pardon my intrusion, your Majesty, is preposterous. They are obviously liars and thieves. We should hang them now, and waste no more of your time."

"He's lying," Mitch sputtered.

"You dare question my word?" Fordyn said. "You are but wastrels and scoundrels. Your Majesty, I beg you to allow me to avenge my honour. Order your guards to run them through."

I felt the point of a spear poke painfully at my back. "No, he's lying," I said. "He—"

The Queen raised her hand again. "There is a way to find the truth," she said. "If this is, indeed, the Talisman, and you are, as you claim, the Guardians, then the Talisman will speak to you." She looked at Ellen. "Give them the Talisman."

Ellen handed it to me. I looked at the black surface and saw only my face. Then the stone began to tingle in my hands and the reflection of my face faded and I thought I was looking into a hole that grew deeper and broader until I felt like I was going to fall into it. From above, I heard the Queen's voice. "What do you see?"

"Fire," I said, my eyes widening as the picture became clearer. "Ships on fire, scattering your enemies, driving them into the open ocean."

When I looked up at the Queen, her smile was gone,

and the white make-up around her eyes was lined with creases. I gave the Talisman to Mitch. A few moments later, he too was staring into it with wide eyes. "I see water," he said. "Waves from a great storm, smashing your enemies onto the rocks."

The Queen nodded her head slowly. "Will it speak to me?"

"Lies and trickery," Fordyn shouted. "This proves nothing."

"The Talisman reveals itself to those it chooses," Mitch said, ignoring him. "But if you have a true heart, it may show you what you need to know."

"It is a deception," Fordyn cried. "They mean to harm Her Majesty. Do not let him give her that stone!"

But Mitch stepped forward and held it out to her and the Queen took it from his hand. "It is now yours," Mitch said. "Use it wisely."

Behind us, the Guards gasped and went quiet, as if they were all holding their breath. I don't think the Queen was used to being talked to like that, especially by commoners. She glared at Mitch, looking like she was ready to order her guards to cut off his head, but then she looked at her hands.

"It tingles," she said, her voice rising in amazement. "I can feel its power." She held it in the palms of her crossed hands, gazing into its black depths. Her breath caught in her throat and, slowly, her mouth formed a perfect "O."

"What do you see, your Majesty," Dudley asked.

The Queen raised her head, her face glowing. She gazed at the soldiers spread out in front of her and smiled. "I see victory," she said. Then her eyes narrowed as she turned toward Fordyn. "And I see that Lord Fordyn is a liar and a traitor. Seize him."

Fordyn yanked the reins and kicked his horse, trying to turn and run, but Dudley's men surrounded him, boxing him in. Dudley galloped forward, snatched the reins from Fordyn and led him away. Fordyn turned in his saddle, shouting to the men behind him. "Attack, you fools! It is not too late. Now is your chance. Do you want a woman ruling over you? A weak leader our enemies can easily defeat? Show your strength! Act now!"

"Silence him," the Queen said. "And return the cloak to its rightful owners."

The guards pulled Fordyn roughly from his saddle. As Fordyn struggled and continue to shout orders to his men, they stripped the cloak from him, tied his hands and gagged him. Across the gap, Fordyn's soldiers raised their lances while their leaders looked from one to the other, fearful of making the first move. They remained uncertain, but ready. If one gave the order, they would all attack.

Then, as the Guard dropped the cloak into Mitch's hands, the Queen urged her horse forward. The Guards parted to let her pass. Dudley trotted up behind her. "Your Majesty," he said. "It is dangerous. You mustn't."

The Queen waved a hand in his direction and kept going. She entered the gap and walked her horse back and forth in front of the men gathered in the field, many of whom wished to see her dead. She stopped her horse in front of them and spoke, in a voice so clear it seemed to be amplified.

"My loving people. I know I have the body of a weak and feeble woman; but I have the heart and stomach of a king. And a king of England too. And I think foul scorn that Parma or Spain, or any prince of

Europe, should dare to invade the borders of my realm, and before I see any dishonour grow by me, I myself will take up arms. I myself will be your general, judge, and rewarder of every one of your virtues in the field.

"We have been persuaded by some that are careful of our safety, to take heed how we commit ourselves to armed multitudes, for fear of treachery." And here, she paused, gazing hard at the men with their swords at the ready. "But I assure you I do not desire to live to distrust my faithful and loving people. Let tyrants fear, for I have placed my chiefest strength and safeguard in the loyal hearts and good-will of my subjects.

"Therefore, I come amongst you, not for my recreation and disport, but being resolved, in the midst and heat of the battle, to live and die amongst you all, to lay down for my God, and for my kingdom, and for my people, my honour and my blood, even in the dust."

A cheer went up, so loud it seemed to surround me. The soldiers, the guards, the Earls, and attendants all cheered. And so did Fordyn's men, who lowered their swords and shouted along with the rest. The Queen, with the Talisman still clutched in her right hand, opened her arms wide, as if to embrace the entire field. Then she waved and walked her horse back toward us, dismissing the soldiers and her guards as she passed.

She halted her horse in front of us. "And whom do I have to thank for this gift?" she asked. "And what can I give in return?"

Before any of us could answer, William bowed low, sweeping his hand as if removing his cap, even though he wasn't wearing one. Mitch stepped close to me and whispered, "Show off."

William stood upright. "I am William Shakespeare,

a playwright."

The Queen nodded. "Have I seen any of your plays, Mr. Shakespeare?"

"No, your Majesty. I fear none of my plays have yet had the honour of a performance. But you have inspired me this day. Henceforth, I shall write plays about our great monarchs, and ascribe to them speeches as inspiring and rousing as your words on this day. You have become my muse, and I could ask no greater gift."

The Queen gave him an indulgent smile. "Well then, Mr. Shakespeare, I look forward to seeing one of your productions soon."

William bowed again and the Queen turned to us. "And you, Guardians of the Talisman, if you be not knights, then who would you be?"

Mitch took a step forward, hugging the cloak in his arms. "My name is Mitch, and this is my brother, Charlie. We are travellers, from the kingdom of Wynantskill."

"Your kingdom must be far away," the Queen said, "for I have never heard of such a place."

"It is," Mitch said. "And we just want to go home."

The Queen looked at Ellen. "And you, young man. Do you wish to return home, as well?"

Ellen looked at Charlie. "Yes," she said.

"Come closer," the Queen commanded. Ellen took a nervous step forward, to stand at the side of her horse. "Your name, young man?"

"Nicolas, your Majesty" Ellen said. "Nicolas Fen. I am from the north. I came to London in search of adventure."

"And did you find it."

"Yes, your Majesty. But it is time to go home now.

Adventures cannot last forever."

The Queen leaned low. "You are wise, young Nicolas. But keep the tales of your adventures alive. They may inspire others like you to step away from the confines of their birth and accomplish great things." Then the Queen winked and said in a quiet voice, "I, too, know what it is like to be a woman in a man's world. I think we have both done well, Nicolas."

Ellen turned crimson, bowed, and backed into me. I had to grab her to keep from falling over. The Queen smiled and sat up in her saddle.

"Arrange escorts for these young men," she said to her guards. "See them safely to their destinations."

DENOUEMENT

MITCH

We started back to London that afternoon. It's not as if we had much to pack, so once our guards got everything ready, we all left—me, Charlie, Ellen, William and Mendel. While we waited, we were given the opportunity to clean up and dress our wounds, and were provided with new, nicer clothes. Our guards were given horses and carts filled with supplies to help us on our journey, and, to our surprise, the Queen rewarded us for our services—with money. A bag of coins—many of them gold or silver—was given to each of us, along with travel documents and an official order, signed by the Queen herself, that we were to be given free passage and not be inconvenienced in any manner.

Since we didn't need money, I gave my coins to William and Charlie gave his to Ellen. She protested, and only gave in when he allowed her to give him a few groat coins as a token.

"With these riches," she told him, "I could buy my own farm, and not have to marry that awful man."

Then she gave Charlie another hug, which made some of the soldiers watching eye them curiously.

By then, the carts were ready, so we climbed on and rolled out of Tilbury.

It was an easy journey and we made it back to London by early afternoon of the following day. William said a quick good-bye to us before rushing back to his playhouse with his newfound inspiration, and newly acquired capital. Then Ellen and Charlie said a long, sappy good-bye to each other, which they had to do out of sight because the guards still thought she was a boy.

I hugged Ellen and she told me she would never forget us, which I didn't doubt, and then she and our escorts headed north, leaving me, Mendel, Charlie, and the cloak behind. We were well rested, fed, and had some supplies with us. Getting to Horsham would be a two-day journey, but there was one thing we had to do before we left.

We had parted outside of the big church where we had first encountered Arthur and the gang, so we knew our way from there. We followed a winding route through the narrow streets, each of us wearing a pack and Mendel carrying his walking staff. Having spent such a long time away from London, the streets seemed smellier, filthier, and more claustrophobic than before. Fortunately, we wouldn't be in the city for long.

In a short time, we came to the rickety building we knew too well.

"Open," was all Mendel said, when Lovell answered his knock.

Lovell peered through the peephole. His eyes

widened when he saw us.

"You! But … Fordyn …"

"Your benefactor sits in the Tower awaiting execution," Mendel said. "If you do not wish to join him, open this door."

The door creaked open. It was daytime, so Lovell was there on his own. When we stepped inside, I saw his money box on the table, and his ledger books open. Lovell cringed, even though Mendel had not threatened him.

"What do you want of me?" he asked, as if fearing we were going to ask for a pound of his flesh.

"Of yours, nothing," Mendel said. "We want only what you took from these boys."

And so, we set out on the road to Horsham, carrying our modern-day clothes in our packs.

Walking the road was soothing. We (or Mendel, at least) had money for food and lodging, and we didn't have to worry about being arrested. I was so at peace I began to feel sad that the adventure was over. And Charlie, of course, was just feeling sad.

"I really liked her," he said to me. This was on the second day, when he finally felt like talking instead of moping around, sighing and staring at the ground. "But she couldn't come with us, and I can't stay here."

"Did she want you to?" I asked.

Charlie sighed. "Yeah. She had this crazy idea that we could get married, and I could help run the farm. Married! At fifteen! I told her the idea was stupid. It might be okay to get married that young where she comes from, but it's not something I could do. And, besides, I'm not a farmer."

When we reached Horsham, we went straight to the wheat field, which had been harvested in our absence.

171

Charlie and I had to scout around for the arrow marker we had left, but once we found it, we easily located the spot in the field where we had appeared.

Knowing we were about to go home was exciting, frightening, and sad all at once. I turned to Mendel. "I guess this is good-bye. Again."

"Yes," Mendel said. "Until next time."

"You mean there's more?" Charlie asked.

Mendel took the cloak and indicated that we should lie down. "The Talisman is with the Monarchy now. It will protect the Land and be safe enough. For a time. But there will come a day when the Talisman will need to be returned to its rightful place in the Sacred Tor."

We dressed in our normal clothes. Charlie put the groat coins in his pocket, then took them out and gave them to Mendel. "These won't come back with me," he said. "At least if you keep them, I may have a chance of seeing them again."

Mendel smiled and put them in his pouch. "You will," Mendel said.

Then he took the cloak from my pack, told us to lie down, and covered us with it.

"And when will that be?" Charlie asked, his voice muffled by the cloak.

"In time," Mendel said, his voice already fading. "In time."

It's late afternoon now, hardly near bedtime, but the journey has worn us out, and lying on the soft earth—with the air smelling of cut hay, and the sun warming us through the cloak—is so comfortable and soothing, I am sure we will fall asleep very soon.

Historical Note

For a man hailed as the greatest writer in the English language, very little is known about Shakespeare.

He was born on or about the 23rd of April 1564 and died on the 23rd of April 1616. He lived in Stratford-upon-Avon, married Anne Hathaway in 1582, had a daughter, Susanna, in 1583, twins—Hamnet and Judith—in 1585, and wrote many fine plays from around 1592 through 1613 (though there are some who claim he didn't even do that).

The period between the baptism of the twins until his arrival on the theatre scene (1585 to 1592) are known as the lost years, as there is no documentary evidence concerning his whereabouts or activities during this time.

It is therefore perfectly reasonable to speculate that he may have been at Tilbury in August 1588, where he heard Queen Elizabeth's rousing speech.

We know for a fact that Queen Elizabeth was there, and we know for a fact that we cannot rule out the possibility that Shakespeare was, as well.

About the Author

Michael Harling is originally from upstate New York. He moved to Britain in 2002 and currently lives in Sussex.

Lindenwald Press
Sussex, United Kingdom

Printed in Great Britain
by Amazon